THE COPSE MURDERS

Simon Ford

Simon A Ford

The characters and events portrayed in this book are fictitious. Any similarity to real persons, living or dead, is coincidental and not intended by the author.

ISBN-13: 9781068448355

THE COPSE MURDERS

Forward

As in the first book in this series, The Woodland Path Murders, I have used a little literary licence in the telling of the following story, both in terms of characters, and places where they play out the action. The settings are broadly based on fact but to fit the story I have embellished or altered them slightly. I ask for the forgiveness of any locals, purists or historians who may take offence at this.

Introduction

Organised crime might appear to be a relatively modern phenomena. The term was certainly not widely used before the middle of the 20th century. However, this is not the case. You could argue that one village raiding another for their corn, or their women, was organised crime. Or one country invading another for their oil or gas resources is organised crime, state sponsored.

Nowadays the initialism OCG refers to any

sort of gang or group that combines personnel in order to commit any number of crimes including drug trafficking, gun smuggling, modern slavery, protection rackets, illegal immigrant trafficking and other crimes, usually for financial gain.

Police Forces throughout the UK have specialised units set up to tackle these criminals who can be very sophisticated in their modus operandi. Good examples are found in London gangs, historically like the Kray Twins and their gang. Peaky Blinders, the TV dramatisation, was based on a real organisation in Birmingham, that operated from 1880 until after the First World War, when it was boosted partially because soldiers returning after the war were not given any help to get back into society and work. They derived their name from the peaked caps they wore. The apocryphal story was that they hid disposable razor blades in their caps and if they whipped the hat across your face, you were more than likely to be blinded by the blade. This is unlikely to be true as Gillette did not bring these blades to market until the early 1900s whereas the name Peaky Blinders was in use from 1880. It is more likely the name was due to the way they wore the caps, over one eye.

Then there is the Mafia. The classic organised crime group, originating from Sicily but now spread all over, particularly in America. It now seems that most countries have their own mafia style organisations, or version of it, despite the only ones that can truly be called Mafia are Italians. The

Russians, the Columbians and even the Israelis have their own versions.

These violent crime gangs like to refer to different factions rather un-quaintly as run by Families. Loyalties and the security of these groups is maintained by threats of, and actual, violence and murder. It seems that there are enough bad people in the world to make these multi-billion pound 'businesses'.

The Yardies originated possibly from the Jamaican Patois 'yard' referring to the Government sponsored Social Housing or simply 'home'. Jamaican immigrants referred to themselves as Yardies and then criminal gangs took on the name, also referring to areas or turf where they operated.

By the 1980s, a drop in Jamaican government budgets resulted in less money being paid by political parties to their gangs of armed supporters. These political Yardie gangs thus increasingly turned to apolitical criminal activity, such as drug trafficking, to bring in income. At the same time, the Jamaican government severely cracked down on Yardie gangs and political violence in general, leading many so-called Yardie gangsters to immigrate abroad and establish gangs in the U.K., U.S., and Canada. The establishment of Yardie gangs abroad coincided with the rise of crack cocaine in both North America and the U.K., and Yardie and Posse gangs from Jamaica became heavily involved in the trafficking of crack cocaine and other drugs, in addition to illegal gambling and other criminal activity.

Such OCG groups are spread all over the country and also have links abroad. The leaders of these groups are very hard to track down as they disseminated responsibility through networks of operatives who, even if caught, do not know who their bosses are and therefore can't turn evidence against them. Either that, or they are too scared of repercussions if they do rat on them.

Arguably, people who run these gangs, and some who are in them, could be classed as psychopaths. They are an ideal environment for people who have no empathy and don't care what they do do get their ill gotten gains. Control and power also feature heavily in the running of these gangs and punishment meted out to those who disobey or step out of line.

They say crime doesn't pay. It's a reflection of life in general really. Those at the top make loads of money and those at the bottom, don't...and usually are the ones that get caught and pay the price for the criminal activity.

A Copse is a small group of trees. There is no defined size or number of trees. The word "copse" comes from the 1570s and it was a contraction of the word "coppice" which was a process of woodland management whereby trees and bushes were cut down to ground level in order to promote new growth. The moniker of a copse is now more widely used simply to describe a small group of trees or shrubs, whether they are actively managed or not.

Coppicing is a sustainable forestry technique

that uses nature's capacity for regeneration to continually harvest wood from a living tree. Many hardwood trees will attempt to regrow after being cut down. Trees like maples and oaks will send up numerous shoots from their stumps, (called a stool if the tree is being coppiced,) which allows for repeated harvests on a set cycle.   When a tree like a maple is cut, the resulting shoots can be thinned, leaving a relatively small number of shoots. These shoots will grow, resulting in a multi-trunk tree. You can harvest these new trunks once they reach the size you need.

Prologue

20 Years Ago

Peter Corrigan swung his legs to and fro whilst sitting on the wall of the little bridge that crossed the small river that ran across the farmland where he lived. He was 16 years old and really didn't want to be there at all. His little cousin Neil really was a little shit. Peter was watching him pull the legs off the frogs that he had caught from the slack water the other side of the bridge.

Did he really derive pleasure from doing that? he asked himself.

His so called cousin was 5 years younger than him. They weren't really cousins but it was a moniker their foster parents had used for simplification. Mostly for telling outsiders about the family rather than for the boys benefit. Neil didn't talk about his background so Peter wasn't aware of what he had been through. He assumed it wasn't great otherwise he wouldn't have been fostered.

Peter's own childhood....he now considered himself to be a man...was peppered with angst, abuse, violence and a lack of any kind of love, tough or otherwise. He was where he was now because he had tried to kill his father the last time he had tried to do the things he had been doing to him for so long, from such a young age. He would understand as he got older that what he had been through was a combination of sexual and psychological abuse.

His father had pushed Peter too far and hadn't realised he had become a strong teenager, who could fight back. He had fought back, big time. He only regretted that he hadn't killed his father, who was now in prison. On investigation, the police had discovered what had been going on and removed Peter from the family home. His mother's testimony had backed him up and helped put his father away, for a long time. There were questions as to whether her previous silence had in some way enabled her husband but eventually it was decided she was under his coercive control. This was becoming much more recognised as a mechanism used by narcissistic personalities.

His parents were called Nancy & Jeff. How ridiculous, they sounded like a sitcom couple. That, they were not. Their surname was Jones but for anonymity, Peter had adopted his foster parents' surname, Corrigan. He didn't mind, it was a much more interesting name than Jones.

His 'new' parents were called Rob and Susan Corrigan and they ran a farm on the outskirts of Warwick. Mostly dairy but with come crops grown in rotation in a couple of the fields they had. They were in their 60s and starting to feel their age. They had fostered 2 young boys, with the hope of eventually adopting them. The other boy was called Neil. The hope was that Peter and Neil would be able to help out with some of the physical duties on the farm. Peter was up for it. It meant he was on his own most of the time. He liked that. Neil, on the other hand, was a lazy little shite.

So far, Peter had managed to suppress the emotional pain of not being loved by anyone. Whatever Neil had been through, he clearly hadn't suppressed anything. It was quite normal for young boys to experiment, e.g. using a magnifying glass to focus sunlight onto an ant to see what happened. But to keep doing it and to progress to bigger and bigger animals...that definitely wasn't right.

"Look Peter, it's still alive" said Neil, waving a legless frog in front of his cousin's face.

"Oh, fuck off you retard" shouted Peter.

He jumped down off the wall and walked away from the macabre scene. He had chores to do so he headed back towards the farmhouse. He enjoyed the physical labour and being outdoors. He wasn't particularly academic so had recently left school, for good. He would learn more and more about farming and eventually take over from Rob and Susan.

As he came through the gate that led from a field to a track that went up to the yard, he saw a black vehicle pulling away and heading down towards the main road. It seemed to pull away at some speed. He wondered who it could be. The passenger window was open and the occupant looked dark skinned with dreadlocks.

As he got closer to the farmhouse he could tell something was wrong. The dogs weren't barking. They always barked and ran around the yard, particularly chasing any vehicles that visited the farm. There was no sign of them.

Peter moved closer to the farmhouse, looking around him as he went. The car had turned out into the main road and had disappeared, at speed. He thought it was some kind of Land Rover 4x4. A Discovery perhaps, or a Range Rover. It was too far away to be precise. He got to the door of the farmhouse which was half ajar. He pushed it fully open and called out.

"Rob....Susan...are you in there? Is everything alright?" he said, nervously.

He saw the dogs first. Both lying motionless on the hall floor. There was no blood. They had probably had their necks broken. There was blood in the kitchen when he looked through the door from the hallway. Lots of blood. All over the kitchen. His foster parent were both on the floor, clearly dead.

His reaction was interesting. All he could think

about was how to clean up all the blood. Then he realised he would have to do something with the bodies. Then the big one hit him. They would come for him and Neil and they would have to go through the rigmarole of finding new homes for them. He liked it on the farm. He wanted to stay. This was going to take some working out.

He did vaguely wonder why they had been killed. Presumably they had upset someone, really badly, or had interrupted a burglary. He didn't think there was much to steal in the farmhouse but maybe they had some cash hidden away somewhere.

Neil. What was he going to tell Neil? He looked out of the window and saw the boy coming across the field, returning home after his frog torturing session. He shut the kitchen door and headed out to intercept the boy.

"Hey, Neil" he called across the yard. "Need a word. In the barn. Now" he demanded.

They converged on the barn that held some old farm machinery and smelled of a mixture of old grease and oil and cow shit. Peter thought about how to tell his cousin. Just come straight out with it, is probably best.

"Neil ... Rob and Susan are dead. Someone broke in and killed them, and the dogs" he said, simply.

"Oh, ok. What do we do now then? I'm hungry" asked Neil. It hadn't seemed to phase him one little bit.

"We need to be damn clever, that's what. If we are going to stay here....I assume you want to stay here?". The other boy just nodded.

"Ok. Well here is what we need to do" said Peter.

CHAPTER 1

Present day.

If DI Chamberlain had been an owl and had been out hunting this night, in these woods, he might be perched in one of many trees. If he was perched in a certain tree he would be looking down on a scene of such horror.

The body of a young male was lying, almost unrecognisable, on the rotting vegetation of the woodland floor. The man was dead, certainly. He was also in pieces.

There was another man, standing slightly to one side, examining his own handiwork. Peter Corrigan was finishing off his latest conquest. He knew this man to be a two bit criminal, part of a gang out of Birmingham. He knew this because he had researched him, followed him and eventually killed him. He deserved it. A worthless specimen of a human being.

He wasn't the first, and certainly wouldn't be the last, if Peter Corrigan had anything to do with it. He wiped the sweat from his brow. It was hard work cutting up a human body. Disposal was easier that way. Transport was easier and burial also. He had learned this many years ago when he and his young cousin Neil, had had to dispose of their foster parent's bodies. They hadn't killed Rob and Susan themselves. No, they had been killed by persons unknown who had appeared at the farm house one day, some 20 years ago.

They were both quite young at the time so dismembering the bodies had been the practical way of dealing with and hiding them. They had buried them amongst the ancient mounds in the woods where they used to play. Nobody used the path that led through those woods anymore so it was an ideal hiding place. Peter had used it again and again ever since.

However, he wouldn't be using the mounds any more. He was resigned to the fact that they would find his original 'stash' but he had been careful not to leave evidence. He had removed all the teeth and fingers of the bodies. In any case, they would most likely blame his cousin Neil.

But the area was now the subject of a major archaeological dig. He had found somewhere else to bury his victims. Not too far away, still in some woods but not the woods where the mounds were located. These woods probably were once connected but since agriculture had split up the land, these new woods were unlikely to be searched as part of the dig.

It hadn't taken him long to decide on this place place. He had used Google Earth to look down on the area that the farm occupied to find somewhere that might be suitable. It was actually quite a small patch of deciduous woodland situated among a number of fields. It was more like a copse really. If you didn't know about it, you were unlikely to stumble across it. Even dog walkers didn't pass near to it. It was a little more awkward for him to transport his waste but he had a system. It was still on land belonging to the farm, so no one would question him driving around in his 4x4.

Now it was time to get rid of the latest victim.

He gathered up the tools of his trade. Very sharp knives, bone saw, strong pliers and a pair of sharp secateurs. He also had a roll of thick black bin bags. He set about packaging up the body parts of the victim lying lifeless before him.

It took him the best part of a hour before he was finished. There were 15 packages in all, containing the body parts, and one more containing the bloody clothing, the contents of which he would burn at the farm yard tomorrow. He loaded the bags into the back of the pick up. On the journey to the woods the victim was alive and in one piece, though unconscious.

Peter Corrigan had found this one in a back street of Birmingham. He had posed as a buyer, looking for drugs. The young black lad had confirmed his suspicions when he offered him a range of illegal substances. Weed, crack cocaine and smack. While he retrieved the goods from an inside pocket, Peter had struck him on the back of the head, rendering him unconscious. It had been easy to put him in the back of the pick up and cover him with an old tarpaulin.

When they got to the woods, he wouldn't kill him straight away. No, he needed information from this piece of shite. The information extraction, and eventual killing, took place far away from the burial site in the copse. Corrigan felt this was a sensible level of precaution. Once abducted the drug dealer was taken by Corrigan to a large woodland area on the other side of the Old Birmingham Road. It was actually Forestry Commission managed land, though legally still part of the farm and was covered in Pine Trees. There were rough tracks that crisscrossed the area and were easily accessible. Whilst popular with dog walkers during the day, nighttime was a different matter. Ideal.

The Forestry Commission was founded in September 1919 to restore the nation's woods and forests following the First World War, which, like the building of the Navy to fight the Spanish Armada hundreds of years earlier, was a huge drain on the forest cover of the country. This resulted in the passing of the Forestry Act. They are England's largest land manager looking after over 1,500 forests. They also deliver internationally renowned research in sustainable forestry and help other landowners make their woodlands more productive, better for wildlife, and prepared for the challenges of a changing climate.

The first patch of forestry was planted in Eggesford in Devon, a mixture of Beech and Larch. Part of the re-foresting process involved helping land owners to plant large areas of land, with financial incentives. This forest was mainly pine trees which were a rotating crop of timber. Some areas contained young trees, recently planted. Others were older trees and would be scheduled for felling and processing.

Peter Corrigan had chosen an area he knew to be in-between these stages and therefore safe for his plans, at least for the time being.

Obviously, the process was messy. Corrigan would rake away the dead pine needles and clear an area big enough for his purposes. Once he had finished, he would rake the needles back over the blooded forest floor. Once it rained, and it did quite often, the blood would soak away into the loam. There was little chance of discovery, and even if a dog got over interested, there was no body to discover.

When he dragged this one out of the back of the pick up from under the tarp, he was still unconscious. That always helped when setting up the next stage of the proceedings. Over the years he had refined his methods, discarding what seemed ineffectual and developing what clearly got results.

The first thing to do was to lay the body out on the earthen floor of the copse and peg out his limbs. This he did with efficiency. However much the man struggled, once conscious and in pain, he would not get free. Also, because of the remoteness of the location, no one would hear him scream. He was very likely to scream, unless he wanted to give up the required information without any pressure being necessary. Time to remove the gaffer tape from his mouth.

"Ahhrgh....fuck, what the fuck, man?" shouted the man.

"Sorry about that...and welcome to my domain" said Corrigan.

"Who are you and what are you doing?" asked the man.

"Both pertinent questions, well done. My name is Peter Corrigan and I am here to get information concerning the identity and whereabouts of your boss" explained Corrigan.

"Huh, you can go fuck yerself mate. I ain't telling you nuffing"

"Ok, we can do this the hard way then. Hard for you, I should say but very easy for me" Corrigan said calmly.

He fetched his bag of tools from his pick up and plonked them down next to the spreadeagled man. He selected a claw hammer and with one swift movement, smashed it down on the man's right knee. There was a sickening crunch and then a piercing scream. Tears ran down the sides of the mans face.

"How's that for starters?" enquired Corrigan.

All that came back were indistinguishable expletives and groans. Maybe he had hit him too hard.

"Ok, sorry, that was a bit brutal for a first offensive. Let's try something slightly less painful" Corrigan grabbed the pliers and moved to the mans feet. He placed the jaws around one of the toes and started to squeeze, gently at first, then harder, until the man was squirming and squealing.

"I'll ask the question again, just so we are clear. Who is your boss and where can I find him?" Repeated Corrigan.

"No fuckin' way!" said the man.

You are going to die anyway Corrigan thought to himself. He wasn't going to tell the man that now as that would remove any incentive to give him the information. He always wondered what went through the minds of his victims at this point.

Many torture survivors report revealing false or inaccurate information since their goal was to satisfy the torturer and end the suffering, not to reveal information. If torture goes on too long, the subject reaches a state of learned helplessness which means they give up any idea of escaping.

In a sense, a brain that has reached the point of learned helplessness is a brain in a near permanent state of torture. The subject loses any sense of a future outside of suffering. If you believe the adage from existential psychologist Rollo May that depression is "the inability to construct a future," then depressive is more than an accurate description.

Torture is, of course, illegal under

international law but Peter Corrigan didn't give a fig for the rules. There was no one to reprimand or stop him, in any case.

"Have it your own way" taunted Corrigan.

He smashed the hammer down on the other knee. Again, a crunch and then a scream. The poor victim was really suffering, more tears pouring down his face. Pain is a strange thing. It is among the most important signals our body gives to help us survive. Pain can alert us to harmful changes in the body, like cancer, or help us learn to avoid something harmful, like touching a hot stove. In this way, some forms of pain keep us safe.

However, when someone else is inflicting the pain and we have no control over the timing or strength of it, unless we are highly conditioned to cope with the onslaught, perhaps as special forces operatives, we tend to try to get it to stop.

Corrigan's victim was getting very close to the point of needing it to stop. He wasn't strong enough to endure the pain to reach the learned helplessness point. He was going to tell him everything he wanted to know.

"Ok....ok, I'll talk!" he said desperately "What do you want to know?"

The next few minutes involved Corrigan asking the questions again and the drug dealer spilling his guts about where he got his supplies from and who his 'boss' was. When Corrigan thought he had all he was going to glean from the unfortunate fellow, he raised the hammer again and smashed it down with great force on the man's head. It killed him instantly.

The next hour or so was spent cutting up the dead body and wrapping the pieces in old newspaper. When he had finished and had put the parcels into black bin bags and loaded them into the back of the pick up, Corrigan spent a few minutes raking dead pine needles over the area in an attempt to hide his work. Looking around, he was satisfied that no one passing by would have any clue as to what had transpired there.

It had taken a while to extract the information but now Corrigan knew where the dead man got his supplies from and the name of the man involved. He wasn't the big boss but it was a start. None of the previous victims had given him any information before succumbing to death. This one had been weaker willed.

Another added benefit was what were quite often thick wads of cash that his victims were carrying. Helped his cash flow no end. The drugs he found, he wasn't interested in. He would dispose of them as soon as he could, down a drain or off a bridge into a river, or sometimes they got buried with the bodies in the freezer.

As he drove away from the Forest, with the window down and the wind blowing through his hair, he thought back to his childhood and the foster parents that had been so brutally killed. *Another one for you, Rob & Susan* he said to himself.

It had taken quite a while to figure out what had happened that day 20 years ago. At first he had thought it was a bungled robbery but nothing had been taken from the farmhouse. Their first priority had been to hide the bodies and clear up the mess. This had taken them two days by the time they had managed to dismember both bodies, wrap them up and then transport them to the woods. Digging up the existing burial mound had been really hard work. Peter had done most of it as Neil was very young back then.

He had come up with what he thought was a really clever plan. Remove the top of the mound, intact if possible, and then dig down to form a grave. Once the bodies were interred, replace the top of the mound and make it look undisturbed. It had worked to a degree, although in the end they had buried the bodies in the commercial sized freezer that they had initially stored them in. They made good as best they could and relied on nature to do the rest. They knew no one ever used the path so it shouldn't be a problem.

Their next issue was to work out how they could continue living at the farm and make sure no one found out that Rob & Susan were dead. This was going to be tricky as whilst the couple hadn't seemed to have any regular friends, the farm was a working one and had deliveries and the usual comings and goings of an agricultural business.

Peter chuckled to himself. They had managed

to con everyone. Their school, the local council, the Tax man. He had become very good at forging signatures, both Rob's and Susan's. It had been very hard work running the farm but they learned quickly. Early mornings bringing in the cows for milking, then setting them out to graze for the day. Then repeating the process at night.

It had irked him that someone had invaded their space and killed his foster parents. Neil didn't seem to give a shit but Peter felt violated. He would spend years trying to work out who might have done this. They searched through all the farm paperwork for any clues but couldn't find anything apart from and envelope with some instructions and plans for the growing of a different crop than they were used to. It would involve the use and fitting out of one of the barns. It was non-specific and obviously Rob and Susan had not pursued the idea.

Then one day, about ten years later, he had read and article in a newspaper.

Suffolk Farmer arrested after discovery of large amount of marijuana growing in barn. Heat signature and excessive electric bill led to discovery. The farmer denied responsibility claiming he had simply rented out the barn to some business men and was unaware of what was in the barn. The business men were from outside the area, possibly from the Midlands, he had said.

This had got him thinking. Had Rob & Susan been approached to rent out a barn and set up a marijuana farm, refused to do it and been punished for their refusal and silenced? He would then spend years searching the streets for drug dealers and reeking his revenge whilst trying to find out who ran the operations in the area.

When a psychopath seeks revenge or runs a vendetta, their lack of empathy and consideration for others intensifies the tendency to ruminate about revenge. Another label for someone might be a 'vindictive narcissist' which is an unofficial term used to describe narcissists who hold grudges, harbour resentment, and seek revenge when they feel wronged. Vindictiveness is understood to be a hostile defence mechanism a narcissist uses when they feel threatened, insecure, or offended by someone.

In some cases, such as Peter Corrigan, it can come down to semantics to a degree and be somewhat subjective. His focus was on the people he thought had killed his foster parents. If that event had not occurred he may never have become a serial killer....then again, he might.

Corrigan came out of the forest and drove a little way down the main road. He then turned off on a barely visible track and drove for about a mile, through fields and farm gates, until he reached the edge of an isolated copse. He stopped and got out of his pick up. Then he went round the back, dropped the tail gate and pulled all the contents out on to the ground. There had been several packages but he had put them into 3 separate bin bags. He hoisted the first one onto his back.

He moved pretty quietly through woods, not as stealthy as a fox but good enough. He had years of practice. The odd snap of a dry twig, the rustle of dead leaves but nothing you wouldn't normally hear at night in woodland. This would be the first in the new burial site so the digging would be hard work. He set to it.

CHAPTER 2

DI Ralph Chamberlain was sitting at his desk in his office at the Warwick Police HQ. He wasn't an owl, of course, though he was a bit of a night bird. He had a habit of staying up late and falling asleep in his armchair with his lit pipe resting on his lap. He had got through several pairs of trousers from the resulting ember burns.

He also burnt the pockets when he was smoking during the day. His old housekeeper, Mrs Frobisher, used to mend the pockets but she had been murdered by the psychopathic serial killer, Neil Corrigan. Chamberlain hadn't replaced her. The basement flat in his house that she used to occupy was lying empty at the moment.

Over the weekend just gone, Chamberlain had taken a rare opportunity to get his fishing gear out of the under stairs cupboard and try his luck on one of the smaller rivers in the area. The River Avon, which flows through Warwick, is mostly a coarse fishing river. Chamberlain preferred to fly fish for brown or rainbow trout. This meant he had to travel out to somewhere like the Blythe or the Alne. He was a member of the Blythe Angling & Conservation

Society, although he didn't have enough time to really take advantage of his membership.

The weather over the last few days had been ok for fishing. Not too bright and dry most of the time. The water level of the river wasn't great and he hadn't caught anything. He didn't mind this. The main benefit he got from spending time on the river bank was the quiet and solitude.

He'd had to renew his Environment Agency rod licence. It was lucky he had checked before he went because it had run out several months ago. It just showed how often he was able to get out on the river. He had a small selection of flies, all barbless hooks and no bigger than size 8. There were rules. He probably should have renewed the fly line on his reel by now as it was over ten years old. He would get round to it one day. It was getting a little stiff so casting a straight line was not easy.

He had chuckled a little at what he must have looked like, The quintessential English Country Gent, out on the river, waders on, pipe in mouth, puffing away mainly for the smoke to keep the midges away. He refused to wear a hat, which would have completed the picture, particularly if he wore a Tilley Hat, the soft head garb of many outdoorsmen and women. He did actually possess one of these but it stayed in the cupboard at home, unless he was fishing at night.

The River Blythe flows through the English Midlands from central Warwickshire, through the Borough of Solihull and on to Coleshill in north Warwickshire. It is quoted as anything between 26 and 45 kilometres long, possibly due to the myriad of waterways in Warwickshire. Even the map makers seemed to get confused. Although it ran quite near to Birmingham, it was surrounded by fields and countryside. It was also within easy reach for a busy Detective Inspector.

On this trip he had taken a paltry pack lunch and a flask of coffee. He loved being by the river. The calming flow of water, the nature that took its' life force from the liquid. He didn't need to be fishing to enjoy it but it helped to distract his frantic mind from the day to day pressures of policing, dealing with criminals and the darker sides of human nature. The whole ritual of setting up the rod, threading the line, checking the leader, selecting a fly for the prevailing conditions...some might say a rigmarole but to a fisherman, this was all part of the enjoyment.

Despite the sewage spillages and leaching of agricultural chemicals, the river systems of the UK were the life blood of a robust population and the backbone of the industrial revolution. Populations, thought the world, grew up near to waterways or the sea, for a number of reasons including food, communication and defence. Fishing for food was no longer a necessity but Chamberlain, along with many, many others, enjoyed it nonetheless.

He had cast his line with unusual accuracy on this occasion. There was a central avenue of faster water with calmer sections either side. A quick upstream mend got the fly running perfectly. He still didn't catch anything. 'There's nay bleddy fush in the river' many frustrated anglers would say. The truth was more likely that there were fish but the water level, temperature and general conditions meant they were not feeding...or that the fisherman was just bloody useless.

Chamberlain didn't mind which it was. He was just happy working his way down the river bank, stopping halfway through the day for his pack lunch and coffee. Afterwards he sat there with a full bowl of tobacco in his pipe and ruminated about life in general. He was lucky in that there didn't seem to be any other fisherman out. Peace.

He thought back to when his father had taught him how to fish. They had gone out together to try their luck on many of the smaller waterways in Warwickshire. His father would have his trusty nine foot fly rod and Ralph had a cheap, Childs rod, bought at a local toy shop. He used worms and maggots in those days, although he had to get his father to thread them on to the hook. They wriggled too much for his liking but his father said it would attract the fish.

And it did. Ralph caught his first fish on a maggot. It was a very small perch but it was a catch all the same. He was very proud of it and wanted to take it home to show his mother and his friends. His father insisted he put the fish back in the stream though. 'You can come back and catch him when he has grown into a big fish, my boy' he'd said.

Ever since, Ralph had been hooked, so to speak, and progressed from worming to fly fishing as soon as he was big enough. He would have to admit that he actually caught more fish on the worm than he did on the fly but it was regarded as bad form for an adult to use worms or maggots for game fishing. In fact, some rivers and waterways prohibited their use. Another change from those days was that you had to use barbless hooks so as not to damage the fishes mouth. It meant you had to play the fish more carefully but it did make sense where the majority of fishing was catch and release.

It was getting late so he packed up and left the beautiful stretch of water, promising himself he would come here more often, fish or no fish. He tried to mentally prepare himself for work the next day.

It was rare that he came into his office, preferring to be outside. However, this morning, he had to finish off some paperwork relating to the Corrigan case. He also had a meeting with his boss, DCI Rebecca Flemming, later in the morning.

The Corrigan case had taken a lot out of the team. It had been a close call and if it hadn't been for Chamberlain's oppo, DS Tom Harris, he may not be sitting here today. Neil Corrigan had Chamberlain and his now girlfriend, Judith Webster, tied up and ready to be killed on the battlements of the Mill House at Warwick Castle. Yes, Chamberlain had managed to break free and had charged into Corrigan taking them both over the battlements and into the River Avon but if Harris hadn't burst through the door at that very moment and jumped in after them, Chamberlain may have died with Corrigan at the bottom of the river.

His girlfriend. He hadn't been expecting to use that phrase, for sure. It had seemed to happen so quickly. Maybe the trauma of the Corrigan kidnapping and subsequent events had thrown them together. A shared terror and close shave with death. Was he ready for this kind of commitment? Who ever was ready? It was early days in any case.

They had all been to the presentation of Harris's Bravery Award a couple of weeks ago. All were togged up in their dress uniforms. Very smart, very hot, very uncomfortable. Chamberlain had watched his Sergeant with an amount of pride. The man should go far, given the opportunity, but Chamberlain did not want to lose him. A selfish thought but there it was.

After his second cup of coffee it was time to go and have his meeting with DCI Flemming. It was an unscheduled meeting so he wasn't sure what it was about. There were no new cases to brief her on. Budget cuts seemed the most likely subject. Always budget cuts. God he could do with a smoke. He fiddled with the pipe in his pocket as he made his way to her office. It would have to wait until after their meeting.

When he had come in to the HQ that morning, there had been an atmosphere, a feeling of impending....something. Chamberlain wasn't sure what. Everyone felt it, no one mentioned it.

He knocked on her closed door, which was unusual. She normally had an open door policy.

"Come in" came her voice. Sounded rather formal to Chamberlain.

"Morning Ma'm" said Chamberlain, to match the apparent mood.

"Take a seat Ralph". He sat. "How's the team doing after all the hoohah?" she asked immediately.

"They're good, thanks. They are a solid bunch to be honest. I am proud of them and proud to work with them" he replied.

"Good, good....and Judith?" she continued.

"Err, well, she's great....but you know that. She calls you all the time and I am sure you get all the gory details" he said without bitterness. He knew how good friends they were.

"Well, yes, quite" There was clearly something else on her mind that she was struggling to get out.

"Is everything alright, Ma'm" he said.

"Oh for God's sake stop calling me Ma'm, at least when it is just you and me" she said. She paused and took a deep breath.

"I have cancer, Ralph. Breast cancer. I have just had it confirmed" she blurted it out at last. She had been thinking of the right way to tell him but in the end, just the plain truth was the best way.

Chamberlain shook his head in disbelief. "Are you sure? Of course you are sure, sorry. How long have you known? he asked.

"I felt a lump a couple months ago. I had a series of tests and scans and they have now confirmed it. Before you get all maudlin on me, they reckon they have caught it early and the prognosis is good. However, I may have to take a leave of absence for some treatment and I will need you to take the reins. You are perfectly capable and the team respect you, so no resistance please."

"No problem, of course M'a....Rebecca." he quickly correct himself.

"This is between ourselves for the moment please, until I know what is going to happen next" said Flemming.

"Of course. Do the top brass know yet?" asked Chamberlain.

"No, not yet. They will only get all flustered and try to get me to retire or take extended leave. I don't want that, at least not unless it is absolutely necessary" she paused, then looked at him. "Judith knows, you won't be surprised to hear. I told her right at the beginning. Don't be cross with her that she hasn't told you. I swore her to secrecy".

That didn't bother him, nor surprise him in the least. Rebecca and Judith had been mates since university and he could imagine that his boss had needed to tell someone, probably even before her husband. Although Rebecca was older, by some years, she had been a mature student at the same time Judith had been doing her Journalism degree, straight out of school.

"I'm so sorry, Rebecca. Anything I can do, just ask. It goes without saying" said Chamberlain. He was shocked but he didn't want her to think he was pitying her. She was a strong, proud woman. She would fight this tooth and nail, he was sure.

Just then there was a knock on the door.

"Yes" said Flemming, sounding exasperated.

The door opened and it was DS Harris. He looked in with a questioning look on his face. One look from Chamberlain and the question on his lips to ask if everything was ok, died before it emerged.

"Sorry to disturb you Ma'm but there is a Gentleman on the phone asking to see a senior detective. He is a solicitor Ma'm" explained Harris.

"We are not holding anyone at the moment are we?" checked Flemming.

"No, we are not" answered Chamberlain, "Did he say what it is about, Tom?"

"No, Sir. But we do know him. It's Frank Williams from Turner, Williams & Crowe, in Birmingham" said Harris.

"Aaaah right, yes, the firm that seems to represent most of the scum bags in the city. Organised crime etc." said Chamberlain.

"Everyone has the right to legal advice and defence" said Flemming.

"Hmphh" grunted Chamberlain. He wasn't so sure, sometimes. "Ok, I'll see him, no need for you to be involved Ma'm" he said, bearing in mind their previous conversation.

"Thank you Ralph" she said.

"Tell him I can see him tomorrow morning, 10am, will you Tom" Chamberlain instructed.

Harris left to organise the meeting. Chamberlain remained where he was for a few moments. He wanted to make sure his boss was ok. She must be going through hell with all this.

"Don't molly coddle me Ralph, I couldn't bear that" said Flemming.

"Wouldn't dream of it" he said, defensively." I'll deal with this solicitor and keep him out of your hair".

"Be nice" she said. He ignored her and left her office, heading out to the car park for a fill of his pipe, wondering what this objectionable man was going to want to talk about.

CHAPTER 3

After the Neil Corrigan incident, the area in the woods where the mounds had been found, and where Mrs Frobisher's body had been discovered, a massive archaeological dig had been organised. It turned out to be quite an important Iron Age settlement. They had found some interesting artefacts in the mounds that contained the old, old bodies, or skeletons as they in fact were. These included some pottery fragments and flint tools. There was a rumour that Professor Alice Roberts, the TV archaeologist, might visit with a film crew at some point.

They had dealt with most of the burial mounds but also had uncovered the remains of ancient walls. These were established to cover an area which suggested it was a small village. The archaeologists were very excited indeed.

They were about to excavate the final burial mound. They were expecting and hoping, to find another ancient skeleton of the same era as the others. What they found was more horror than historic. This mound contained a large chest freezer which contained a whole load of body parts, some in skeleton form, some still with flesh on them, albeit in advanced state of decay. The latter were obviously relatively recent, though older than the other bodies they had already attributed to Neil Corrigan.

They appeared to be all wrapped up in newspaper but one or two of these had split open, revealing the contents. Before fully excavating the multiple burial, Richard Bewley, the senior CSI, put in a call to Warwick Police HQ for DI Chamberlain.

“Inspector, it’s Richard Bewley. I think you had better come out and have a look at what he have found. I’ll warn you, it’s pretty gruesome” he told Chamberlain.

“Ok, Richard, we’re on our way” Chamberlain replied. “Tom, with me, you drive” he shouted across from his office.

“Where are we off to, Sir?’ asked his Sergeant, whilst grabbing his jacket off the back of his chair.

“Back to the mounds Tom, back to the mounds” he sounded like a character in a Tolkien movie.

They headed to the car park. Chamberlain already had his pipe out ready. With Tom driving he could concentrate on getting a bowl of his favourite pile tobacco, Capstan Navy Cut, into the bowl and lit so he could puff, puff, puff.

As they drove out to the Old Birmingham Road, for the umpteenth time, they remembered why they had been called out there in the first place a few weeks ago. Two poachers had been found dead by the farmer, part way up a little used path through a piece of woodland. It turned out to be a personal message to Chamberlain from a 'looney killer" as his boss's friend Professor Phillips had referred to Neil Corrigan.

Corrigan had held a grudge against Chamberlain for many years due to the young PC interrupting one of his 'projects'. He wanted revenge and in the process had killed Chamberlain's housekeeper, Mrs Frobisher, and nearly killed Chamberlain himself and the journalist, Judith Webster. She was now Chamberlain's girlfriend. It sounded very teenagerish to call her that but he didn't mind. It was still early days to call it anything else.

They approached the lay-by that gave access to this end of the footpath but they drove past and headed for the other access track. It would be easier to get to the scene via the other end of the path.

They parked up at the gate at the top of the farm track. There were a few vehicles belonging to SOCOs and also to the archaeologists which had been parked on the other side of the gate in the field itself. Chamberlain got out of the car and fished his pipe from his pocket. So far, no holes in these trousers. He lit up and them started to walk along the edge of the field towards the stile that led to the top end of the path. DS Harris followed him.

It was a clear day, only a few wispy clouds in the sky. Harris had to walk through the haze of pipe smoke as he followed his boss. It wasn't an altogether unpleasant smell. Harris had got used to it, working with this man as long as he had.

They had a good team, led technically by DCI Rebecca Flemming but in reality, on the ground, his boss was DI Ralph Chamberlain. He had joined the inspectors team a couple of years ago and had soon settle into his boss's ways, for example, he knew his boss wasn't keen on being in the office, preferring to be out on the streets, or in his satellite office, as he called the cafe around the corner, where he could think more clearly. He could also smoke his pipe when he was out of the office.

Harris had recently found out that his girlfriend, Madeleine, or Mads as he called her, was pregnant. After the initial shock, and discussions that persuaded him he didn't have to marry her immediately but that it was something to think about for the future, they were talking about potential names for the baby. There was plenty of time but they both had somewhat different ideas on the subject. She favoured something modern whereas he wanted a more traditional Warwickshire name for the boy or girl.

As he walked along the field edge he was wondering how he could persuade Mads that his choice of name was better than hers.

"Some chance" he said under his breath.

"What's that, Tom?" queried Chamberlain.

"Oh nothing Sir, just thinking out loud" Harris replied. He hadn't realised he had said it loud enough to be heard.

"Thinking about impending parenthood, are we?" taunted Chamberlain.

"Something like that Sir" said Harris. How the hell did his boss know what he was thinking? "It's just that we have been talking about names and we can't agree on anything yet" he explained further.

Chamberlain stopped abruptly. "Hmmm, good luck with that. What you need to do is plant a seed and develop it so that she thinks it was her idea." said Chamberlain.

"Right. Not sure she would fall for that but it's worth a try"

The two men continued in silence. Chamberlain was thinking about his own situation and life choices. He had no children, as yet. Was it too late for him? Probably not, as men were capable of reproducing well into old age. Was Judith someone he would want to have children with? Would she want children, seeing as she had a career of her own? Lots of questions without answers at the moment. He envied his sergeant who seemed to be following the classic path towards having a family.

DS Tom Harris, on the other hand, was thinking whether he was ready for such commitment. Were either of them? He loved Mads dearly and certainly wanted a family with her. He thought she felt the same but how could one ever be sure? Statistics were not on their side, for sure. He wondered whether humans were really designed for long term relationships. Or was he just too cynical?

They got to the stile and both stopped abruptly, realising they had been miles away, metaphorically, in similar directions, but at some distance from the job in hand.

CHAPTER 4

Stan Hemmings was a bastard. He knew it, everyone knew it. He wanted it that way. Keep everyone scared of him, that was the way to keep control. That wasn't his real name. He was a 'Yardie'. He was part of the diaspora of Jamaican settlers who had come from the Caribbean in the 1960s. He was only a young child then and didn't remember Jamaica but he was very proud of his heritage.

His real name was Adio Johnson. Ironic, seeing as Adio meant 'be righteous'. He used Stan Hemmings as his business name. He called it business. Everybody else, including the Midlands Police Force, called it Organised Crime. He'd been doing it for a long time now and he had seen some changes over the years. His business front was a repair garage. He was actually quite a good mechanic, having learned as an apprentice when he was old enough after he came to England. His main, and more lucrative, business was drugs distribution.

He was now in his early 60s and not as physically capable as he used to be. He used his minions for that side of the business nowadays. That could range from a minor roughing up all the way to offing someone completely. He had a whole network of distributors, or soldiers as he liked to call them, who operated mainly in the midlands but the reach was sometimes as far as Suffolk to the East and Manchester further north. He had to be a little careful not to encroach too much on other gangs' patches. That could mean war. He didn't mind a bit of fighting but usually it was better to maintain the status quo.

However, despite all the bravado and his ever strong conviction that he was the boss, he was in charge, he was feeling increasingly worried. He kept losing soldiers. This wasn't just a case of people moving on or moving away. Natural wastage was inevitable but they were disappearing without any trace at all. At the last reckoning he had lost 7 of the crew. Was someone trying to muscle in on his 'Yard'?

"Wah di fuck gwaan?" he said to his 2IC. His closest lieutenant was a scrawny little runt simply called Big John, or BJ for short.

"Mi nuh kno boss" came the reply.

"Mi cyaa kip losing gud men, man" complained Hemmings.

"Mi kno, boss, It a mystery fi sure" said BJ, shaking his head.

The Jamaican Patois would have been a little tricky for an outsider to understand but that was partly the point. They had known each other for many, many years and the trust worked both ways. Neither man trusted anyone else in the same way. They had grown up together, had fought side by side, had laughed together, cried together. They were like brothers although they were not related.

"Cum wi hope di solicita comes up wid sup'm" said Hemmings.

Like most organised crime groups, they had a tame solicitor who was happy to take a retainer and be on hand if Hemmings, or any of his crew, needed legal representation. This was quite often, so the brief found the arrangement quite lucrative...morals be damned.

Stan had tasked this solicitor with going round all the CID offices within a certain radius, asking if they had any bodies turn up that couldn't be identified. It was a long shot but he was running out of ideas. The solicitor had better hurry up. Stan wasn't a patient man. And at the moment, he was a worried man. This could lead to rash decisions and indiscriminate recriminations. He knew who his competition was, at least in the immediate area. He could make them suffer. Oh yes, he certainly could.

BJ had lit a large spliff, taken a few drags on it and handed it to Stan. This was a regular habit, a ritual. They smoked so much of the stuff that they were almost immune to the effects. It was part of their life, their culture. No one was going to tell them they couldn't smoke the weed, not even the bizzies....especially not the bizzies.

Stan leaned back in his chair and said languorously “Mi a guh kill di bastard that doing dis”.

BJ nodded, sagely.

The two men sat there for a while, just enjoying the feeling of the drug they were inhaling. It was actually quite a long while as time tended to lose its’ meaning after a certain amount of weed. They used a lot of it but it wasn’t their main source of income, not their main product.

No, that was crack cocaine. The market for the drug had ballooned since the 1970s and 80s and was now a multi-billion pound supply industry. They had their share of the market and were determined to keep it, if not increase it. For that, they needed distributors. Someone appeared to be getting rid of their distributors and they needed to put a stop to it.

Oh, there were plenty of potential recruits on the streets but that meant having to train them up and instil the loyalty that he demanded. That all took time. Added to that was the threat that some one was out there, targeting his crew.

Stan came to a decision. He needed eyes on the streets in case the solicitor had no luck. He would call his senior lieutenants in for a meeting and explain the plan to them. They wouldn’t like it but he didn’t care about that. They would do as they were told, or else.

“BJ…arrange a meeting wid di senia distributas” he said to Big John.

“But boss…” started BJ.

"Jus dweet!" shouted Stan.

BJ knew not to push a point, despite their close relationship. He wasn't happy with the idea, their business relied on as little contact as possible between the various units of the gang. Safer that way. However, if his boss wanted a meeting, his boss got a meeting. He pulled out his phone and scrolled through the contacts.

CHAPTER 5

Chamberlain and Harris climbed over the stile that led from the field to the path. It hadn't been long since they had been here the last time when poor Mrs Frobisher's body had been found. They made their way down the path to the area with the burial mounds. The whole area was an archaeological dig now. However, all work had been suspended while the final mound had been investigated. There were mounds of excavated earth dotted about, sorting tables with tools on them. A small marquee had been erected in one corner of the clearing.

As they approached they saw the unmistakable figure of a CSI, all dressed up in protective gear. They knew this would be Richard Bewley, though they couldn't see his face. It had been him that had rung Chamberlain to ask for him to attend the scene.

"That's far enough" shouted the figure when he saw them. They weren't wearing any protective gear and might contaminate the scene. "I'll come to you Inspector. And put that damn pipe away, will you, please" he added.

Chamberlain had the offending item in his

mouth, though it had now gone out. He removed it and put it in his pocket. No need to upset the fellow. They waited for the spectre to make his way towards them.

"So, what have you got for us, Richard" asked Chamberlain.

"Where to start!" came the reply. "We thought there would either be an ancient skeleton or a newer body, or possibly both. However, what we have here is a whole new ball game. Parts. Body parts. Lots of them. And how they are concealed under the mound is, if I may say so, rather inventive".

Chamberlain and Harris both looked bewildered and intrigued at the same time. Quite a picture. Under different circumstances, Richard Bewley would have been quite amused.

"Whoever created this clearly had used it over a period of time and wanted to keep it accessible. They have somehow maintained the integrity of the mound on the surface and have buried a large chest freezer underneath it. It's not quite full but not far off it. At this stage, I have no way of knowing how many bodies there are contained in the freezer. In fact, no way of telling if all or any of the bodies are complete. This is going to take some considerable amount of time Inspector."

"Wow, ok, can we get a closer look?" asked Chamberlain.

“If you can be bothered to get suited and booted, then yes” replied Bewley. “Or you can wait for the SOCO photographs. I really just wanted you to get a feel for the scene, in the flesh...ha ha sorry, no pun intended...and understand how much would have gone into organising this”.

Chamberlain couldn’t be bothered to suit and boot. The photographs would do, along with the description from Bewley. The immediate assumption was that this was all down to Neil Corrigan but Chamberlain knew the danger of making assumptions.

“Bloody hell, Corrigan was a busy boy then wasn’t he sir” said Harris.

“We can’t know this is definitely Corrigan’s work at this point, Tom” said Chamberlain “Remember, follow the evidence”.

“But that would be a hell of a coincidence if this was down to someone else wouldn’t it, and you know what they say about coincidence.”

Chamberlain hated it when people dramatically said there was no such thing as a coincidence. Of course there was. That was why there was a word for it. This would be a huge one, he had to admit but nonetheless, they would have to consider it. His first thoughts were that this MO was very different to the other murders by Neil Corrigan.

"Ok, I think we have seen enough. Not much more we can do until Forensics and Pathology have done their stuff" said Chamberlain.

He and Harris made their way back up the path, over the stile and along the edge of the field to the gateway where they had parked, among the other official vehicles. There was also now a large tractor, pulled a little further into the field itself. On the tractor was Peter Corrigan.

"Didn't expect to see you up here again, Inspector" he called out from his perch.

"Just ongoing enquiries Mr Corrigan. You know what these things are like, always take longer than you think" replied Chamberlain.

"Ain't that the truth" said Corrigan. He put the tractor in gear and drove off towards the other side of the field. *A strange one* thought Chamberlain to himself. But then he guessed being a farmer, you were on your own a lot of the time.

The two policemen got into their car and drove off back down the track to the main road and headed back towards Warwick town centre and the police HQ. In the short time they had been in the woods, some workmen had set up on a stretch of the main road, including traffic lights at each end of a stretch of road that was particularly bad for potholes.

Of course, the lights turned red just as they arrived at the start of the bollards. They waited....and waited. Finally the lights turned green and Chamberlain pulled out to follow the signs. This involved driving over quite a few cats eyes with the associated gthump gthump gthump.

Chamberlain started to say "You know that's how...."

"Cats eyes get cleaned. Yes, I know that sir" interrupted Harris.

"Ok, smart arse. Do you know the name of the man who invented them?" countered Chamberlain.

"No but I am guessing you do Sir?" said Harris.

"No idea" came the reply. "But I do know he was a Yorkshireman and he made a fortune out of the invention. Millions of them all over the world now".

"Fascinating" said Harris, sarcastically. In fact, as he wasn't driving, Harris was surreptitiously Googling the invention from his iPhone. "Percy Shaw's the man you are talking about sir" he said triumphantly.

"That's the fella" said Chamberlain.

"It says here he got an OBE for it but went a bit eccentric in his old age, removing carpets and curtains from his house and leaving TVs on all over the place on different channels. Sounds like a nutter to me" said Harris.

"Nutter he might have been, Tom, but his

invention must have saved countless lives all over the world".

They drove on further, in silence, heading for Warwick centre and the police HQ building.

CHAPTER 6

Judith Webster had been going to see a psychotherapist since her ordeal at Warwick Castle with Neil Corrigan. She hadn't told anyone, especially not Ralph. In some twisted way, she felt guilty for having to go to these sessions. Would Ralph think it was his fault? Getting her embroiled in his work and putting her life in danger. She didn't think anything of the sort but she kept her visits to Dr. Samantha Howard to herself.

Today was her fifth visit and she was looking forward to it. The last time she had seen Dr. Howard she had left feeling quite elated. The first session had been difficult. Dr. Howard was a stranger and had asked Judith a lot of personal questions. That had brought back feelings and emotions she had tried to bury. However, for the next couple of sessions they had not mentioned the kidnap at all. She had relaxed and more able to open up to the therapist. The sessions appeared to be working.

When she got to Dr. Howard's therapy room, which was actually the front room of her end-of-terrace house in a quiet part of Leamington Spa, she was slightly late due to the traffic. She realised this would eat into her session time as Dr. Howard was always busy and had a full diary.

"I'm so sorry I'm late Doctor" she said as she arrived.

"No worries, Judith. And please…I think you should just call me Sam. We have got to know each other well enough, don't you think?" said Howard.

"Ok, Sam it is then" said Judith cheerfully. She liked the woman very much.

They both went into the therapy room and took seats on a comfortable sofa. There was no big desk for Sam to sit behind and no couch for Judith to lie back on. There was a low coffee table with very little on it except for a notepad and pencil for Sam's use during the session and a jug of water and two glasses.

"How have you been since our last meeting then?" said Sam.

"Pretty good actually. I am feeling a lot less insecure at the moment" answered Judith, looking around the room and realising that she had never really taken in her surroundings before, despite having been to the room several times.

It was subtly and tastefully decorated with walls painted a very pale blue shade of white. It made the room bright without being clinical. There were a few large pot plants in the corners. The floor was polished boards with a large rectangular rug in the middle of the room which added some warmth. The pictures on the walls were rather nondescript abstracts with lots of colour and merging shapes.

Sam interrupted her thoughts. "You mentioned before that you are seeing someone...a certain heroic detective" It was a statement but Judith recognised that it was really a question.

"Am I fixated on the person who saved my life, do you mean?"Judith said, almost accusatory. Sam just smiled and waited.

"No, I don't think so. We had started with a few dates before...you know...the thing" she said, whilst questioning herself in her mind. She looked down into her lap.

"It's ok to mention the event rather than calling it 'the thing'. And I am not accusing you of anything, just encouraging you to think about yourself after what must have been a very traumatic experience" said Sam.

"I will admit that the fact Ralph saved my life certainly earned him several brownie points but I was already attracted to him before ...the kidnapping" she finished, deliberately.

"Ok, let's leave that for now then. I'm pleased for you actually. It gives you someone to talk to about it and someone who was involved so will know exactly what you are talking about and what you went through. Have you told him yet about our sessions?"

asked Sam.

"No, not yet" said Judith. She hadn't felt ready to tell Ralph she was seeing a therapist. It felt private, though she wasn't quite sure why it should.

"I think you should tell him now. You don't want him to find out another way and think you have been keeping things from him. That's not a great start to a relationship. Judith knew she was right.

"I'll think about it" she said, for now.

They chatted some more....in fact, Judith chatted mostly. She seemed to get on a roll and told Sam all about her fears and foibles, some of which went back to childhood. Not that she had had a bad upbringing. To the contrary, she had always felt happy and secure. It is true though that parents do spend quite a lot of time scaring the living daylights out of their kids....a form of coercive control really, whether it's the monster under the bed to get them to stay in bed or other such mind games.

Judith suddenly realised something.

"I've been gabbling on and you have hardly said a word" she said.

"Absolutely. This isn't about me. It is my job to nudge you into talking about your inner feelings and emotions. Once you have vocalised these, you will find them easier to deal with. The less I say, the better" Sam answered.

"I do feel relaxed and able to talk freely" said Judith. "It's not what I expected from therapy. I suppose I had in my mind a serious professor with a pipe, talking over me lying on a couch" she laughed.

"I don't smoke a pipe I'm afraid" joked Sam.

This made Judith immediately think of Ralph and she wanted to see him and talk to him about it all.

"I'm afraid times up for this session" Sam said.

"Blimey that went quick" said Judith.

"Time flies etc....Just to give you a bit of a heads up, Judith, next time I want to actually talk about the kidnapping itself, in detail. Productive as these last few sessions have been, we haven't got down to the nitty gritty, as it were" Sam warned Judith.

"Oookay" said Judith, rather hesitantly.

They booked up the next appointment and Judith left. She felt exhausted but less burdened. She decided she would tell Ralph about her therapy sessions.

CHAPTER 7

Chamberlain was due to meet Judith for dinner. He was getting ready, like a love sick schoolboy. He had showered, re-pressed his best shirt, and made sure the trousers he chose had no holes in them from pipe burns. He had also trimmed his moustache and brushed his hair perfectly. He wasn't really vain but he knew that Judith would be looking stunning and be dressed up to the nines. To be honest, she looked stunning whatever she was wearing....*or not wearing* he thought to himself and grinned.

He didn't usually wear any pungent deodorant but tonight he applied a tiny spot of aftershave on his neck. It was a brand Judith had recommended and he had bought some. He paused...he wondered if it was a subtle way of telling him that the smell of his pipe smoke was too much. No....she would have said it outright, she was that kind of person.

As he went towards the front door he glanced down the stairs that led to the basement flat where Mrs Frobisher had lived. Her loss was still raw. He had done nothing about clearing the flat of her belongings. He reflected that the garden was also going to need attention. This had been one of her tasks. It hadn't been part of the work brief but she seemed to get a lot of joy out of doing it so he had let her carry on.

He missed their little chats, her scolding him occasionally about the pipe burns. They would share a pot of tea from time to time, usually in her little kitchenette downstairs.....

He pushed these thoughts aside and left the house, locking the front door behind him. He felt for his pipe and then thought the better of it. Maybe he should arrive at the date without the lingering smell in tow. He was due to meet Judith at an out of town restaurant, on the road towards Leamington Spa. She still didn't feel comfortable being in Warwick itself.

She was there already, waiting for him, 20 minutes later. She was dressed up and she did look stunning. In his usual self-deprecating way he wondered why the hell she was attracted to him.

"Morning!" he greeted her.

"Morning?" she queried. "It's 7.30 in the evening".

"Sorry, stupid habit. It is morning somewhere though!" he retorted.

"Ha, well I guess it is. Let's go and have some breakfast then, shall we?" she said with a grin.

They took their seats at a cosy table for two. It was a Japanese themed restaurant. Chamberlain wasn't sure if he like this kind of food but he hadn't admitted that to Judith. He was looking worriedly at the menu.

“Don’t worry Ralph, I’ll chose you something fairly innocuous. I can see you are not familiar with Japanese dishes” she was grinning again. How did she do that? She seemed to be able to read his mind. Female intuition or some such hocus pocus.

“No, I’m not a mind reader or a witch. I asked Rebecca about your tastes in food”.

DCI Rebecca Flemming, who was his boss, and Judith were long time friends and Chamberlain should have known there would be an almost constant line of communication open between them.

“Ah yes, my boss and my girlfriend are besties. Excellent.” he said with some concern. ”Do you tell her absolutely everything?” He was now thinking about their more intimate moments.

“Of course....oh, the sex, you mean. No, don’t worry. I haven’t compromised your professional relationship that far.” she said.

He visibly relaxed, his shoulders dropping to a more natural level. He wouldn’t be able to look Rebecca in the eye if he thought she knew what they got up to in that department, though he was pretty sure her imagination would leave little to question. If he had only known how right he was. DCI Flemming had definitely noticed him walking taller, with the air of a happier man, recently.

"Do you cook much for yourself?" asked Judith.

The implication, whether intentional or not, that he was a sad, lonely bachelor, was not lost on Chamberlain and he smarted slightly.

"I can cook...but I wouldn't say that I am that interested in cooking. It is tricky catering for one and I find there is often quite a lot of wastage. Mrs Frobisher would occasionally make something up for me.....anyway, yes I eat a lot of ready meals" he was a little defensive.

"I know what you mean. I am similar. I do love watching cookery programs but I very seldom copy the recipes" she said.

"You know what annoys me about those programs?" he said, and continued without waiting for an answer "I just wish TV chefs would stop saying 'this is a super easy recipe'."

"Yeah, easy for them maybe" she agreed, "My pet hate is when they say 'Use whatever you have in your store cupboard'. They clearly haven't seen what's in mine!" They both laughed at this.

True to her word, his dish, when it arrived, was delicious. Some kind of fish with a slightly spicy sauce and Japanese vegetables. She had some sushi selection. To accompany the food they had a very cold, dry Pinot Grigio. They talked easily during the course of the meal, no desserts but coffee to finish off with.

It was really good coffee and Chamberlain just couldn't stop himself. It came out almost like a mantra.

"Ahhh Bisto" he said.

"What? Gravy?" said Judith, raising her eyebrows.

"Sorry, you might be too young to remember the Bisto Kids. I can't stop myself saying it if I have a nice drink. Silly really" explained Chamberlain.

"Bloody daft!" she corrected him. They both laughed it off and carried on drinking the coffee.

"So, are we a couple, then...officially?" said Judith.

He thought about it and in a moment of bravery, trying to emulate her candid approach, said...

"Well, we have had sex now. I assumed the next step was a full white wedding" he hoped he hadn't overstepped the humorous approach.

"Absolutely" she threw back at him. Her expression was serious.

"Ah, bugger, well what I meant was...." Chamberlain stuttered.

She burst into hysterics and couldn't speak for about a minute. Eventually she could breath again.

"Nice try, but don't try and kid a kidder" she said. "But seriously, we have been thrown together under unusual circumstances so let's just take it as it comes and see what happens. I like you a lot, Ralph Chamberlain, and that takes a lot for me to say, believe me".

Chamberlain visibly relaxed. He liked her a lot but he agreed they should move slowly. They weren't love struck children and didn't need to launch into the usual paradigm of youthful exuberance and commit to each other right now, without actually getting to know each other properly.

It had occurred to Chamberlain that because of their very different jobs, there could be times where their motivations and loyalties could clash so they would have to be very careful about that if they were to have a future together.

They went dutch on the meal and because they both had heavy work loads they went their separate ways. If they had gone home together, either to his or hers, they knew they would not get much sleep.

Judith realised later that she still hadn't told Ralph about her therapy sessions. It had just slipped her mind. Well, that's what she told herself anyway.

CHAPTER 8

Chamberlain walked into his boss's office the following morning.

"You ok Ralph?" She could see his forehead was furrowed. Clearly he had something on his mind.

"Am I too old for Judith?" he said.

"Don't be a twat" came the immediate reply.

"Thanks... helpful" said Chamberlain. He had been thinking about it most of the night following their meal together.

"No, seriously, you're not too old. Don't the French say that the ideal age for a man's partner is half his age plus seven?" she said.

"Well, in that case, she is too old for me!" He had quickly worked the sum and his ideal woman would be 27-28, according to the French. Judith was early 30s.

"I wouldn't go telling her that, if I were you" warned Flemming.

"No, I won't, though she seems to be able to

read my mind" complained Chamberlain.

"Yes, she is a canny lass, and no mistake" said Judith's friend, proudly. "Listen, Ralph, on a more serious note, how are you coping over the death of Mrs Frobisher? I know you were very fond of her and the manner of her death must give you nightmares."

"I do miss her, very much. And not just because she did the cleaning and the garden" explained Chamberlain. "It's very sad, and horrific. That bastard just used her to get my attention".

"You should speak to someone about it. If not the force therapist, then someone from outside" said Flemming.

"Nah, bollocks, I don't have time. You know what we have to deal with now they have made the latest discovery. It's a right meat puzzle, apparently" said Chamberlain.

"Charmingly put" replied his boss. "Ok, but think about it, when you have dealt with this case. For Judith's sake as much as anything" she cautioned.

"I'll think about it" he replied "Now I want to go and talk to your other friend, Professor Phillips"

"I do actually have more than two friends you know" said Flemming, defensively.

"Sure" he replied and left her office.

He had already arranged a meeting with the

Professor and made his way to the car park. It was only a half hour drive, at most, to the University where the Professor worked. Not a long journey but plenty of time to have a bowl of his favourite pipe tobacco.

Back in her office, DCI Flemming grinned to herself. She was really pleased that Ralph and Judith had started their relationship. She was very fond of them both, in different ways perhaps but fond just the same.

Then she remembered her own troubles which all of a sudden hit her in the guts. She felt a little light headed at the thought of what was to come. More tests, possible surgery....there was the risk she wouldn't make it at all. Her thoughts turned to her family. Her loyal husband. Her almost grown up children. They would be fine, eventually, but she couldn't help thinking about all the things that *she* would miss out on if the cancer did kill her.

Her phone rang. It was reception to tell her that a solicitor had arrived to see DI Chamberlain but they couldn't find him.

"Oh for fucks sake Ralph" she said under breath. He had clearly forgotten about his agreed meeting with this man and gone off to meet her friend Professor Richard Phillips. Perhaps he had deliberately forgotten.

"I'll go and see him" she said reluctantly.

Frank Williams was waiting in the meeting

room, looking a little nervous if the DCI was honest.

"Mr Williams. I am DCI Flemming. DI Chamberlain has been called away on urgent police business I'm afraid" she said.

"Ok, no problem. I'm sure you can help just as well" Williams replied.

"Ok, how can I help?" she asked.

"Yes, well, I represent certain clients…" he began.

"We know exactly who your clients are Mr Williams" interrupted Flemming.

"Right. Well, these clients have some serious concerns and have asked me to make some enquiries with the police" he started. He was clearly nervous. If DCI Flemming was any judge, she would guess his clients had asked him to do something that he really wasn't't keen to do. She was right.

"What concerns would those be Mr Williams?" she asked. She wasn't aware of any current cases involving his clients and they definitely didn't have anyone in custody at the moment.

"Well, the thing is that they have noticed that they keep having members of their crew disappear. Seven so far, to be precise" he explained. "And my client wondered if you might have had any unidentified bodies turn up around here" There, he'd said it. He physically relaxed.

“That’s quite a jump from disappearing to being a body, don’t you think? And why in this area in particular? asked Flemming.

“Oh, no, I am going around all the forces in the area asking the same questions” he blurted out.

“Are you, by jove” said Flemming. This was sounding like it was going to be a huge waste of her time. Chamberlain would get it in the neck for landing her in this situation. “I’ll get a PC to come in and take some descriptions and details from you” she tried to fob him off.

“Ah, well, you see, I don’t have any information to give. The, err, nature of my clients business means that many of the workforce are autonomous and aren’t known personally to him” Williams was really nervous again.

“So, not a lot to go on then, is there Mr Williams” Flemming was getting mighty frustrated now. This meeting needed to come to an end.

“Leave your contact details and I will make some enquiries. If I find anything then I will let you know”. She went to leave the room.

“Thank you. I’ll let my client know. He will be very pleased with your cooperation” said Williams.

DCI Flemming had no intention of making any

enquiries. She wasn't the personal police force for a scum bag drug dealer who had lost some of his runners, whatever the reason.

Frank Williams went away feeling only slightly better than when he arrived. He knew he would have to have the same conversation with several other DCIs in the West Midlands area. His next port of call was going to be Coventry. He didn't know the city that well, other than the fact it had been bombed heavily in World War 2 and had a new Cathedral for its' trouble. He idly wondered where the saying 'sent to Coventry' came from. He knew it meant people wouldn't talk to you but why Coventry?

When he got to his car, he Googled it. Apparently the phrase originated from a 17th century English Civil War punishment, when Coventry was a Parliamentary stronghold. The king's soldiers were so hated that Royalist prisoners were sent to Coventry, where it was felt they would be ignored. It was probably not a fact he would retain in his memory. He had more important things to worry about.

He had noticed that he wasn't getting many enquiries for his legal services any more. He wondered if people knew he was retained by a big OCG boss. The retainer was healthy but he had no way of knowing how long term the arrangement might be. What would happen if he was dropped all of a sudden? He had no real business base to fall back on. He vowed to do something about it when the current business blew over.

CHAPTER 9

The greeting Chamberlain got on his arrival for his meeting with Richard Phillips rather took him aback. He felt he was sponging off the Professor and taking advantage of his generous nature, and making the most of his friendship with DCI Flemming.

"Inspector, how wonderful to see you again. Do come in and have a seat" said Phillips.

Chamberlain got over the shock of the greeting but wasn't quite sure where he was going to take a seat. All available surfaces in the Professor's office seemed to be taken up by piles of books and papers. The Professor saw his confusion and moved a pile of books from one of the chairs.

"There you go" he said. Chamberlain took a seat.

"I'm hoping you have some more conundrums for me. That last case was a welcome diversion from academia, I can tell you" said Phillips, enthusiastically.

"Well, I may well do, Professor" said Chamberlain. "There has been another major discovery, and whilst it is at the same site as before, my gut tells me there is something different about this, or these, I should say".

Chamberlain went on to explain about the excavation of the final mound and the discovery of the chest freezer containing multiple body parts. The Professor's frown got deeper with every aspect of the discovery relayed by the policeman. When he had finished, there was a pause. Both men sat in silence, Chamberlain waiting for the Professor to give some sort of reaction. After a while the academic spoke.

"From what you tell me, Inspector, I would say you have a very different MO on your hands which suggests another perpetrator. This one appears to be much more organised in the disposal and more deliberate to disguise the burials. You say you are still waiting for forensics and pathology but I suspect you will find that none of the bodies were killed at this location. It is possible they were dismembered where they were killed in order to facilitate easier transport".

"Shit....sorry, it's just that we all thought the Neil Corrigan case was all done and dusted. It would have been much easier for us if these other bodies were just additional ones he had killed".

"It is still possible but doubtful, I'm afraid" said the Professor. "Either a massive coincidence or you have two psychopaths knowingly sharing a disposal site. Now that is scary and a very rare phenomena. I have never come across it before but never say never".

"Is there anything peculiar about killers who cut up the bodies of their victims?" asked Chamberlain.

"Well, ease of transport and disposal are the obvious ones but it could indicate a particular hatred of the victims so they may have been targeted for a reason rather than at random" explained the Professor.

Chamberlain knew that the Professor didn't know all the answers and that any answers he did give came with a huge caveat. They were always based on conjecture, and the limited information that he, Chamberlain, was able to give to the Professor. At this stage, it was very little.

"Ok, maybe we could talk again when I have more information available. I must reiterate how grateful I am for your time, by the way" he told the Professor.

The Professor waved his hand in the air "No problem at all. As I say, it is a nice diversion from the every day".

"Just one more question, if I may, and it relates to the previous case of Neil Corrigan"

"Sure, what's on your mind?" said Phillips.

"It's just that the finale, for want of a better phrase, was very reckless and flamboyant. Why didn't

Corrigan come for me in a more subtle, covert way?"

"It's possible he knew he was going to get caught and even further, maybe he welcomed it. It's not an uncommon feature with Serial Killers" said Phillips. "His overriding purpose appeared to be revenge for events that happened a long time ago and time had allowed these feelings to boil up to such an extent that he lost control of his need for self-preservation. You know, the internal mechanisms... by which I mean the brain or the mind, if you want to distinguish between them... by which we make decisions, either snap or deliberated, are largely unknown though much studied and there are many theories. Conditioning certainly takes a role".

"Interesting" said Chamberlain.....then he suddenly remembered something. "Shit, sorry, I must make a call". He thanked the Professor and excused himself. On the way back to his car he rang his boss, DCI Flemming. He'd only gone and forgotten about the bloody solicitor he was supposed to be meeting back at HQ.

"Rebecca, I'm so, so sorry. I forgot about Frank Williams" he said apologetically.

"Yes, you did. Several minus house points for you DI Chamberlain" she scolded him. He knew she was cross as she had used his official job title, not his christian name like she usually did.

"Fair" he said. "What did the guy want,

anyway?"

"Oh, some bollocks, don't worry about it. You have enough on your plate" she said. She was never very good at being cross with him for long. If she had seen the way Chamberlain was smirking on his way to his car, she might have thought differently.

CHAPTER 10

Stan Hemmings, aka Adio Johnson, was struggling with a particularly stubborn CV joint that needed replacing on an old Rover 3500 . The meeting with his Lieutenants had been fractious but he felt he had got his point across and they were all now aware that there might be danger out in the field for them and their crews.

"Fucking ting!" he swore as the spanner he was using slipped and he scraped his knuckles. It didn't bother him really. He was used to his knuckles being red raw but usually from hitting someone in the face several times. He was in a hurry to finish the job and get out on the street. It had been a while since he had been on the front line but he was determined to get to the bottom of the current situation.

"Yuh alright boss?" came the voice of BJ from the back office.

Yea yuh lazy likkle cunt Stan thought to himself.

"Yea. Just gimme a han wid dis one" he shouted back.

BJ had been rolling another spliff in the back

office and it was planted firmly between his lips as he ambled across to where Stan was working on the old classic.

"Wah di problem boss" drawled BJ. He was pretty stoned. He actually spent most of his life in various degrees of drug induced stupor. Mostly from weed but also other, stronger drugs, like heroin aka smack which is a highly addictive opioid derivative. Frequent lines of cocaine also entered his system through his nose.

All this meant that he was pretty much useless most of the time. Stan was used to it but every now and then he need the waster to give him a hand. He loved the man like a brother but he was frequently frustrated by the state he got himself into. He looked at him now and realised it was pointless asking for his help.

"No, nuh worry mate, mi get it" he told him.

In fact he decided it was time to stop what he was doing, frustrating as it was. He had said the car would be ready by the end of the week. That was looking unlikely now. Well, that was tough shit. He had more pressing things to sort out than a ropey old car. He climbed out of the pit where he had been working, wiped his greasy hands on an oily cloth and discarded it into a bin.

"Cum wi go" Stan summoned his 2IC and they both got into the black Range Rover Vogue that was parked just outside the workshop. Stan liked the vehicle, not just for the image it portrayed, it also was a reliable motor and provided a certain amount of protection out on the streets. This was partly due the manufacturers spec. But also due to the toughened glass and extra side panels he had fitted to the vehicle.

They drove out into the streets of suburban Birmingham and went in search of some of their crew. Stan wanted to check that they were following orders and moving around in pairs. It was for their own protection. He had impressed upon them all at the meeting that this was potentially serious shit. He hoped that they had taken heed.

As they drove around the A4540 which was effectively a ring road, through residential areas and light industrial parks, Stan looked across at BJ. He had passed out. *Useless madafucka* Stan thought. He jabbed him in the ribs.

"Uh, wah dat for?" said BJ indignantly, coming suddenly out of his stupor.

"Mi need yuh tuh tell mi weh di boys likely tuh be" barked Stan.

He hadn't been out on the streets for some time so he wasn't aware of where the dealers plied their trade these days. BJ suggested they try down near the University. Plenty of demand for coke from the students so that was a fairly good bet apparently. There were a couple of railway stations either side of the University that made ideal pick up points, as long as you kept out of the way of the CCTV cameras.

They continued on in silence, mainly because BJ seemed to be finding it difficult not to fall asleep. Stan was thinking he needed to do something about the habits BJ had fallen into. Ok, a few joints now and then and maybe a line or two of coke from time to time but BJ seemed to have slipped into a regime that involved too much, too often. It was affecting his ability to concentrate and therefore to be Stan's number 2. In this business you couldn't afford to be sloppy or off your game if you wanted to survive.

Either BJ would have to change or Stan would have to find another 2IC. That would be a difficult conversation. He loved BJ like a brother but there were limits. BJ had exceeded those limits a long time ago now.

They carried on driving around the outskirts of Birmingham and every now and then BJ would give some directions and they would end up in some back street or other. Sometimes they had to wait a while but eventually BJ would recognise a lone figure ambling down the pavement towards where they were parked.

"Heh, yuh bowy, cum yah!" BJ would shout.

Reluctantly, the boy, or girl, would saunter over to the vehicle, looking shiftily around to make sure no one was watching. BJ would spend a few minutes explaining to the unfortunate that they must now go around in pairs as they might be in danger if they were on their own. None of them liked the idea. They preferred to work on their own and didn't like to rely on anyone else. However, they were mostly savvy enough not to disobey their immediate superiors, especially when they saw who was driving the vehicle. Stan Hemmings's reputation preceded him. You just didn't cross that man.

It got late so they decided to call it a day and head back to the workshop. Besides, BJ had run out of weed and he needed a smoke. They had covered most of the nearer areas but they would have to go further out to catch up with some of the distributors.

CHAPTER 11

"You know I said that this was going to be complicated? Well that doesn't cover it by any stretch of the imagination"

Chamberlain was standing in the autopsy room, looking at what looked like lots of joints of meat, spread out over all four of the available tables. The smell was overpowering, despite the mask he was wearing.

The Pathologist, Professor Daniel Reed, appeared to be in a state of confusion. This was unusual for him. His slightly eccentric autopsy assistant, who wore a bow tie and thought he was Dr. Donald 'Ducky' Mallard from the American TV series NCIS, was also standing in the room with no apparent purpose or direction.

"Ok, well, do you have anything for us at all?" Chamberlain tried not to show his frustration but was pretty sure he had failed.

"Of course I have got something" Reed said indignantly. "But you are going to have to be patient if you want the whole picture here, Inspector". If he sounded curt, he had meant to.

"Sorry Daniel, I didn't mean to be so brusque. It's just been very frustrating, thinking we were done with Corrigan....and now this lot" he said, looking at the various body parts displayed before him.

"I know what you mean, believe me" said Reed. "What I can tell you is that there appear to be 9 dismembered bodies amongst this lot. Seven of them I would guess have been buried for anything from 1 up to a maximum of about 10 years. Two of them have been there much longer, maybe 20 years but no longer. I can be specific about that because of the date on a piece of newspaper in which one of the feet was wrapped".

Chamberlain very quickly realised the significance of the professors last statement. Neil Corrigan would have only have been about 10 or 11 when the first two bodies were buried. Was it likely that he had started killing that early?

His thoughts were interrupted. "There's something else" said Reed.

"Ok, let me have it" what other surprises did the pathologist have for him, thought Chamberlain.

"Well, it's not so easy to tell with the older bodies due to the level of decomposition but the fresher ones are dark skinned, suggesting Afro Caribbean origins. I will need to send tissue and bone samples to forensics for fuller results of course" said

Reed. "Another interesting aspect is that some of them had quite large amounts of drugs buried with them. Much more than would be for personal use"

"You think they could be drug dealers then?" asked Chamberlain.

"Not for me to guess, for you to prove" said Reed.

"I imagine causes of death would be impossible given the state of the bodies" said Chamberlain.

"Actually, maybe not. All of the newer skulls have trauma to them. Not just cracked but with large holes in them. This is likely to have been their cause of death. The older two are more difficult so will need more investigation. I can't tell you anything else at the moment but I hope that gives you food for thought" Reed concluded.

"It certainly does Daniel" Chamberlain replied. He thanked the professor and took his leave, relieved to get out into fresh air. The first thing he did was light his pipe. The strong smell and taste of the Capstan Navy Cut tobacco would alleviate the pungent smells from the autopsy room. This was indeed going to be a puzzle.

His next port of call was Forensics. He made his way there, many thoughts going through his head. When he got there, Richard Bewley, the senior CSI, was leaning over with his head inside a large chest freezer. Chamberlain assumed this was the one in which all the body parts had been buried. It was dirty and bashed about.

"Hi Richard" said Chamberlain, mostly to the man's backside.

"Ah, Chamberlain" came a muffled reply. The man raised himself out of the freezer. He was wearing a sophisticated breathing mask. Chamberlain could imagine why.

"This is fascinating" Bewley went straight into it. "The staining on the inside of this freezer darkens the deeper in you go. It matches the amount of time each body, or bits thereof, have been inside it. Fascinating." he said again. "There is bleed of course....ooh, appropriate pun...but there are almost layers that you can follow"

Chamberlain wasn't sure any pun could be appropriate but he let it pass.

"What can you tell me about the freezer itself, Richard?" he asked.

"Yes, right, well it's a discontinued model from no less than 25 years ago and no more than 30. Not an expensive make but quite large for a domestic freezer. I would say more of a catering or commercial type. Large capacity of about 600 litres, according to Ducky here's calculations. Most domestic ones are under 400 litres apparently. It's pretty beaten up but then it has been in the ground for quite some time. There are parallel marks on the bottom that suggest it might have been moved using a forklift truck or tele handler at some point" explained Bewley.

"Or tractor?" queried Chamberlain.

"Yes, indeed, quite possible" said Bewley. "I'm afraid that is about all we have for you at the moment. It's covered in both Corrigan boys fingerprints, inside and out but it would be if it came from the farm. They don't identify who put this in the ground"

"Ok, thanks Richard. Let me know anything else that pops up" said Chamberlain but Bewley already had his back inside the chest freezer so Chamberlain left. He needed to get back to his team and let them know what had been discovered so far.

CHAPTER 12

Judith Webster had been trying to complete her article, based on her ordeal with Neil Corrigan, the kidnapping, the rescue etc. She was conflicted. Should she, for the sake of completeness, add in the part where she ended up sleeping with the Detective in charge of the case and who was responsible for her rescue?

Or, should she keep that part private and respect his professional integrity? Perhaps she should ask him. Or better still, she would ask her friend Rebecca who just happened to be Ralph's boss.

Her editor had told her there was no hurry. The essentially sensationalist headlines that had reported the outcome of the case had already appeared so there was no rush for what would be a personal interest story. She wanted to get it right. It could lead to greater things and advance her career.

She wanted to appeal to a more discerning reader than the emotive language that had already appeared regarding the Corrigan case. It had read...

Looney serial killer kidnaps our girl who is rescued by hero cop...

She hadn't written that one. Certainly not Pulitzer Prize material. However, she hadn't got very far with her own piece, having only written the title.

She got up from her writing desk and half closed the lid to her laptop. She needed coffee and maybe a chat to Rebecca. Kettle on then. Once she had the steaming mug of milky liquid she settle down on the sofa and dialled her friend.

"Hey you, how are you feeling?" DCI Flemming had answered immediately when she saw who was calling.

"I'm ok thanks. Had a lovely meal out with Ralph last night but we weren't late, it being a school night" she said, trying to pre-empt the probing questions she knew she would get about her and Ralph's love life.

"Yeah, sure, of course" Rebecca didn't believe her but chose not to pursue the matter. "What can I do for you today then, madam?"

Judith wanted to tread carefully and didn't want to put her friend in an awkward position. Yes, she was her friend but also Ralph's boss and a senior police officer.

"Well, I am sat here trying to write an award winning piece about what happened to me. I have got as far as the title and I am not even sure I like that" said Judith, sounding exasperated.

"Maybe it is too soon, do you think?" came the reply. "It could all be too raw for you to write an intelligent article about something so horrific. You were nearly killed for fucks sake....pardon my French...and are probably still coming to terms with that".

"Maybe. But I feel like I need to write it now, as part of the whole 'dealing with it' thing, if that makes sense" said Judith.

"Yes...and no" said Flemming. "Have you spoken to Ralph about this?"

"We've talked about the events themselves but not about this article. That was another thing I am worried about. Should I be talking about our relationship in the article or is that going to compromise his career?" asked Judith.

There was a pause on the other end of the phone. Flemming was giving this some thought.

"I'll speak to Ralph, and you should speak to him as well. For god's sake don't spring it on him when it appears in print" came the eventual advice.

"Ok, will do. I am sorry Rebecca, I should be asking how you are. My problem is trivial compared to yours. How are you feeling? Any more news?"

"Thanks for asking. I have an appointment with a surgeon to discuss options but that isn't for another 6 weeks. Lots of waiting around as usual" said Rebecca.

"Bloody hell, Becca, can't you go private? Won't the force help out?" Judith was angry on her friends behalf.

"You'd think so, wouldn't you? They offer lots of moral and psychological support but nothing very practical I'm afraid" said Flemming.

They chatted a bit longer about more mundane things and agreed to meet up for coffee once they had both spoken to Ralph.

Judith ended the call and returned to her laptop. Her coffee was now a little tepid but she drank it anyway. Maybe the caffeine would wake her thoughts, loosen her fingers and help her to start writing. It didn't. She decided she would ring Ralph later and talk to him about it. No point in just sitting there staring at a computer screen.

She fancied some fresh air but wasn't sure she had the courage yet to go for a walk on her own. It never used to bother her but since recent events she had lost her self-confidence. This, apart from everything else, made her angry. That madman, Corrigan, had taken away her freedom and she wanted it back.

Then she had a thought. Maybe she was trying too hard to write the article, desperate to make it an award winning piece of journalism. Perhaps she should just start by writing down the facts and see what other thoughts came to her in the process. Release the pressure she was self-imposing and perhaps the floodgates would open.

She went and sat down at the table and opened up her laptop. She opened up a new document, didn't yet give it a title but just started typing. Forty five minutes later she stopped and realised she had written nearly 1000 words. She also realised she was starving hungry. She saved the document simply as 'Draft' and closed the laptop. She would get something to eat and would go back to it later and read what she had written. She felt positive.

She didn't eat. She had half a bottle of white wine, a crisp Pinot Grigio, and fell asleep in an armchair. When she awoke, she felt groggy and dry mouthed. A pint of cold water later, she felt better and went back to her laptop. She read through what she had written earlier and became frustrated again. She realised that although she had written a lot, it read like a police report. Just facts, no emotions. She deleted it.

CHAPTER 13

Now back in the incident room, Chamberlain had summoned his team. That included DS Harris and DCs Norrish and Dixon but also a couple of borrowed uniform officers.

He had just updated them on what had happened with the last mound and the contents thereof, including the unusual amount of drugs found. There were mixed looks of shock, dismay and disbelief. There were mutterings.

"I know, I know, we all thought we were done with the path in the woods. However, it seems not. Somehow we need to establish whether these bodies are connected to Neil Corrigan, or if we have a separate killer" Chamberlain said.

"Sir, surely for it to be another killer, it would have to be a massive coincidence that they used the same disposal site" It was DC Dixon. She was proving to be a bright young Detective.

"You're right, it would, but they do happen. Bear in mind that if there are two killers using the same place, they might know each other and be using the site by mutual consent" Chamberlain suggested.

More mutterings ensued. "I need you all to go back over the Neil Corrigan files, statements, forensics etc and check we haven't missed anything. I'm going to go and have another chat with our friend Mr Jones in that pub, whatever it's called"

"The Bell & Tankard, Sir" said Norrish. "Rob Jones is the barman".

"Yes, thank you Norrish" replied Chamberlain.

He then went off out of the HQ and headed for the pub in question. It was walking distance and plenty of time for a smoke. As he walked down Northgate Street and into Church Street he looked across at Warwick Castle. Just the sight of it sent a shiver down his spine. It was the scene of the showdown with Neil Corrigan. How different things could have turned out. If that metal hoop hadn't come loose....if his Sergeant hadn't burst in at the appropriate moment....if, if, if....

He thrust the thoughts aside and brought his mind back to the current situation. If they had another Serial killer out there, they would be starting from scratch. A new case. If they could link the bodies with Neil Corrigan, yes there would be lots of work involved in identifying the victims and notifying ext of kin but they would not be looking for anyone else in connection with the murders. Sod's law told him he was grasping at straws.

He arrived at the door to the Bell & Tankard and went inside. It was not busy, just a few lunchtime drinkers. Rob Jones was behind the bar, chatting to a couple of men who looked like they were right at home sitting at the bar. He went over and got Mr Jones's attention.

"Inspector Chamberlain. Good to see you again" said the barman.

"Morning Mr Jones. I wondered if I could have a quick chat. A couple of things to clear up" said Chamberlain.

"Sure. This lot are all happy so I can spare a few minutes I reckon" replied Jones.

They went across to the same table as the last time Chamberlain had needed a little chat'. He noticed there was no offer of a drink or even a coffee. Community spirit only went so far, he guessed.

"How can I help this time. I thought the serial killer was caught, and killed, in fact, by you, Inspector" said Jones.

"We have another line of enquiry that may or may not be connected to the last case. Can you remember if Corrigan ever came in here with anybody else?" asked Chamberlain.

"Ooh crikey. I don't think so but then I wasn't always here. Shift patterns you understand" he explained.

"Is there anyone else I could ask about that?

Staff, customers?"Chamberlain pressed.

"Oi, do you think he had an accomplice then?" asked Jones, adding 2 and 2 and making at least 8.

Oh shit, here we go again thought Chamberlain. That was going to be splashed across the local papers tomorrow if this man's track record was anything to go by. He tried to pour oil on very bubbling waters.

"We have made no such assumption at this time, and please Mr Jones, do not go to the papers like you did last time, despite me asking you not to do so" accused Chamberlain.

"What do you...." started Jones in protestation. He stopped when he saw the way Chamberlain was looking at him as he knew he had been rumbled. The story about the *Tragic Poachers Feud* had been down to him when Chamberlain had inadvertently let slip that the two murders may not have involved anyone else. The story had appeared the next morning.

"Just promise me you won't repeat that mistake Mr Jones" said Chamberlain.

"Right you are, Inspector" said a very much humbled Jones. He went on, in an attempt to be helpful. "You might try later and speak to Verity. She's on tonight and will be here at the same time as the after work club boys. They might have have seen something".

"Ok, will do. Thank you Mr Jones. That's all

for now". Chamberlain shook hands with the man and left the pub. As he went out through the door he could have sworn he heard the word *Tosser* said under Jones's breath. Oh well, he never signed up to be popular.

Maybe he would go and have another chat with Peter Corrigan, Neil's older cousin. He would have to walk back to the HQ carpark for his car in order to make that visit. He would also pick up Tom Harris to take with him.

There was a slight drizzle now in the air. Chamberlain wished he had a hat, or raincoat. He had never really been one for hats. In his opinion, he had never found a style that suited him. He liked the idea of them, and the practicality on days such as this but alas, he was currently hatless. He quickened his pace.

When he reached the HQ building he was a little dump but not too bad. He collected DS Harris and they headed out towards the Old Birmingham Road once again. Chamberlain could probably drive it blindfold now.

"So, how is Madeleine?" he asked Harris.

"Yeah, pretty good actually. She was expecting all the morning sickness stuff but so far, touch wood, she has been ok. A little tired, that's all really" replied Harris.

"Good, good. I hope that continues. And the name thing?" Chamberlain knew there had been warm, if not fully heated, discussions about what to call the baby.

"Still under discussion" Harris said sheepishly.

The windscreen wipers were now squeaking as the drizzle had eased off. Chamberlain switched them off.

"So, what's our approach to Peter Corrigan, Sir" asked Harris.

"Well, good point. I'm not sure really. I just think we need to ask a few more questions now that we have the latest discovery. I think we may be missing something, though I don't know what exactly" Chamberlain explained.

They drove on in silence for a while. Harris was now thinking about baby names and Chamberlain was trying to figure out how to approach this farmer. He had only had cursory conversations with the man so far. After the death of his cousin, Neil Corrigan, Peter had retreated back to the farm and continued with the daily life of running an agricultural business. As he had stated at his cousin's funeral…'That's that, then'.

He hadn't seemed particularly upset. Maybe they weren't that close. Farming was a tough way of life. The realities of death were there all the time, supposed Chamberlain, though with livestock rather than humans. The circle of life.

Eventually, they arrived at the farm. They hadn't made an appointment so it was possible Peter

Corrigan might not be at the farmhouse. He could be anywhere on the farm. They needn't have worried. There was a figure across the yard fiddling with some machinery. Chamberlain wasn't sure what it was for but it looked pretty lethal with sharp prongs sticking out of it.

They got out of the car and approached the figure. It was Peter Corrigan, in work overalls, oily black hands and smudges all over his face. He swore, loudly.

"Fucking thing, get in there!" he shouted. He was clearly having trouble with said machinery.

"Hello, Mr Corrigan? Can we have a word" said Chamberlain.

Corrigan swivelled round and stared at them, for a moment his eyes looked peculiar, thought Chamberlain. Then he smiled.

"Ah, hello Inspector. What can I do for you?" he said.

"We could do with a quick chat. Just some follow up questions. Routine really" said Chamberlain, rather feebly trying to make light of it.

"Oh, right you are. Let me clean up a bit and we can have some coffee" Corrigan pulled out a dirty rag from his pocket and rubbed his hands vigorously. This appeared to be the sum of his cleaning up as he gestured to the farmhouse and they all trooped into the kitchen.

Chamberlain and Harris sat around a grubby looking kitchen table while their host organised 3 mugs of coffee. The rest of the kitchen wasn't in much of a better state than the table. There were dirty dishes in the sink. Chamberlain noticed a couple of piles of newspapers in the corner. Probably for lighting the coal fired range to the side of them. Coffees delivered, Corrigan sat down with them and looked enquiringly at DI Chamberlain.

"Mr Corrigan, were you close to your cousin Neil?" asked the Inspector.

"Not really, to be honest. Hadn't seen him much these last few years. We grew up here when we were fostered and when we were a bit older, he used to help out around the farm. His heart weren't really in it though. And we aren't really cousins as such, you know" said Corrigan.

"Oh? Did we know that Harris?" Chamberlain asked his sergeant.

"Err, I don't think so sir. I don't think our background checks got very far before....well, you know" answered Harris.

"You can say it, lad. Neil is dead. You won't upset me by saying it" said Corrigan. "We were fostered from different families at the same time and Rob and Susan, our foster parents, thought it easier to describe us as cousins".

"What happened to your foster parents?" asked Chamberlain.

"Oh they are long gone, Inspector. It was hard for Neil and me at first, having to run the farm after they had gone but we soon learned. If we needed help we hired in casual workers, like" explained Corrigan.

"And how big is the farm?" Chamberlain continued.

"Ooh, about 300 acres or so but quite a lot of that is woodland" Corrigan explained.

"And did your cousin display any signs of behaviour that would indicate he was going to turn out as he did?"

"He could be a bit weird as a child, messing about with frogs and other small animals" said Corrigan.

"Messing about?" queried Chamberlain.

"Pullin' their legs off and seeing how long they lived....that sort of thing. Other than that, not really. I assumed he had grown out of it, like many young lads do, like" said Corrigan.

Chamberlain noticed Harris wincing as he took notes. Corrigan was right. Small boys could be incredibly cruel, experimenting with living things. They didn't all turn into psychopathic serial killers though.

"Did you know anything about where he came from? Family history and so on?" asked Chamberlain.

"Not really, to be honest. He would clam up if I ever asked him. I assumed the memories were too painful for him to talk about" came the answer.

Chamberlain had taken a couple of sips of the coffee in front of him but discretion became the better part of valour and he decided he wouldn't drink any more. Harris hadn't touched his at all.

"Ok, thank you Mr Corrigan. I think that is all for now. We will be in touch if we need any further information" Chamberlain decided they probably wouldn't get any useful information from this man. The two policemen got up and went outside. As they were walking towards their car, Chamberlain turned around and saw Peter Corrigan standing at the door, looking at them with a stern expression on his face.

"When we get back, Tom, can you get Norrish and Dixon to finish off the background checks on the Corrigans, and the history of the farm as far back as possible" Chamberlain was a little spooked. He didn't know why, but there it was.

CHAPTER 14

Meanwhile, Norrish and Dixon were heading to the Bell & Tankard to seek out Verity, the bar girl. It was now late afternoon and some of the after work club were already there, in little groups. There was a girl serving one of the customers. She was maybe mid 20s, pretty, long hair tied up in a ponytail.

The two Detective Constables approached the bar and waited for her to become available. She finished serving and came over to them.

“Evening guys, what can I get you?” she asked, looking from one to the other.

“Er, nothing thanks. DCs Norrish and Dixon. Could we have a quick chat?” said Dixon.

“Oh...yeah, the boss said you might pop in. How can I help” she was bright and bubbly and seemed happy to answer their questions.

“Do you always do this shift...er, Verity isn’t it?” said Norrish.

“Yup, usually. I have another job I do in the mornings, have a break and then come in here ’til closing time. Only Monday through Thursday, mind" said Verity.

Norrish pulled out his phone and showed her a photograph of Neil Corrigan first.

"Do you remember seeing this man?" he asked.

"Hmm, yeah, vaguely. I think he used to sit on his own at the end of the bar, over there" she said nodding towards the other side of the room.

"Did you ever speak to him" asked Dixon.

"Not beyond taking his drink order, to be honest. He was very quiet. Just seemed to sit there and watch and listen to the other people around him. At first we thought he might be an undercover cop, you know, checking us out for under age drinkers and so on" said Verity.

"You say, at first. What changed your minds?" asked Norrish.

"Dunno really, he just seemed a bit creepy, you know?" she said.

Some would apply that to coppers thought Dixon.

Norrish looked at his phone again and got up a picture of Peter Corrigan and showed it to the girl.

"How about this guy" he asked.

Verity thought for a moment, concentrating on the image.

“Yeah, maybe...actually yes I do remember seeing him. I think he is the guy who asked a couple of our regulars where he could buy drugs. Everyone thought it was weird, he just didn’t look the type” she said.

Dixon knew it was a daft question before he’d started asking it but it came out anyway. “Do you get much drug dealing in here then?”

Verity just looked at him quizzically and he knew that even if they did, she wouldn’t tell him.

“Was he a regular?” asked Dixon, moving swiftly on.

“Not that I am aware of. I only remember seeing him a couple of times. He was in here not so long ago trying to flog some cows and tractors” answered Verity.

“Ok, thanks for your help” said Norrish. The two policemen then left Verity to her work and exited the pub.

As they walked up the road, Dixon plucked up the courage to say what she had bee thinking for a while.

“Are we ok, mate?”

“What do you mean?” answered Norrish.

“We work ok together right?” enquired Dixon.

"Yeah....sure we do" Norrish answered, quizzically "Why?"

The truth was that Louise Dixon fancied Adam Norrish, a lot, but she was trying not to. This wasn't working, so currently, she was desperately trying not to show that she fancied him.

"Well, sometimes you just seem a bit distant... even dismissive" she said, looking down at the ground and watching her feet move one in front of the other. This was a mistake as she walked into a young lad coming the other way who had his head in his phone. She stumbled a bit and Norrish grabbed her arm to steady her.

"Oops, sorry" she said to the boy. He muttered some expletive but. She couldn't be bothered to pull him up on it, after all it was partly her fault. The two detectives carried on walking along the street.

DC Louise Dixon was sort of seeing someone at the moment but things weren't going very well. She would have to admit her heart wasn't really in it. Her so called boyfriend seemed to prefer to go to the pub on a Friday night rather than take her out on a date. She should probably end the relationship and she realised that familiarity breeds contempt. She shouldn't just stay with him because it was convenient. She new that Adam Norrish was single but she also knew that he was desperately focussed on progressing his career in the police force. He probably didn't want some silly little girl chasing after him. It would probably also be frowned upon professionally, to have a relationship with such a close colleague. Her thoughts on the matter were interrupted.

"So, what did you think of Verity then?" asked Norrish.

"She seemed pretty honest to me" replied Dixon.

"Yeah…me too" agreed Norrish.

"But did you see the guy come out of the toilets, sniffing and rubbing his nose?" asked Dixon.

"Yup!" said Norrish.

Meanwhile, back in the office at the pub, Verity was trying to make a quick phone call. There was no answer.

CHAPTER 15

Stan and BJ were still driving around looking for 'distributors' of their merchandise. They had caught up with a couple of teams and they were following orders and going around in pairs as they had been told, for their own safety. The day was getting on and Stan noticed that BJ was getting a little twitchy. He probably needed another fix.

"Wi check pan one more an den guh home" said Stan, not expecting any reaction from BJ. "Maybe wi cum out again tomorrow an guh furtha out"

All he got in reply was a grunt. He started to head back to the workshop. Maybe he would come on his own tomorrow as BJ was being of little use to him in this state. They arrived back at base and Stan got out of the vehicle. BJ was completely sparko. He left him there. Serve him right.

The next morning, Stan checked the car but there was no sign of BJ. He must have woken in the night and got himself home. Stan didn't bother to check. He had things to do before he headed out to do some more checking on the troops. He had another delivery due in soon. He had to make sure he had enough storage space. The merchandise itself didn't take up much room but the disguised packing cases it arrived in were quite bulky. He had a 20 foot shipping container buried behind the workshop, the entrance to which was well hidden.

There was a wreck of a car parked over the container. All you had to do was lift the bonnet and a trap door was exposed which led down through a hole cut in the roof of the buried container. When lifted, the trapdoor led to a set of steps that took you down into the storage area.

Stan thought this was pretty neat but he also remembered how tricky it had been trying to position the hole for the container in the first place. He had borrowed a digger so actually digging the hole wasn't a problem. However, avoiding the drains and buried cables and pipes had been a nightmare. He had come very close to severing a large electric cable on the first attempt.

Eventually he had found a clear area big enough to accommodate his container. He used battery lanterns to illuminate the storage. It wasn't pleasant being down there for very long but it was only for storage so it was usually a quick in and out job.

As well as his drug store, Stan had a cache of weapons down there. He didn't very often carry. It was too risky. Being of his ethnicity meant he was more likely to be stopped and searched. He kept the weapons hidden and brought them out only if there was a specific threat. He had a couple of shorn-off shotguns and 3 hand guns. There was also plenty of ammunition for all of the weapons.

When he got down into the unit he was pleasantly surprised to find it was very tidy and in order. BJ must have had a session in readiness for the next shipment. Maybe he wasn't as useless as Stan had been thinking after all.

He went to the shelf with the firearms laid out neatly. He picked up one of the hand guns and played with it in his hand, weighing it up and pretend aiming it at nothing in particular. He was trying to decide whether or not to take one with him, especially if BJ was not around to come with him.

He thought about it for a moment and then decided he wouldn't go armed after all. He replaced the gun on the shelf. He didn't like to carry a weapon unless for a specific job. A decision he would later regret. He exited the container and closed the trap door then replaced the bonnet of the wrecked car. Time to get out on the road. He tried BJ on his mobile. No reply. Probably still passed out in bed, the lazy sod.

Stan got into his precious Range Rover and fired up the diesel engine. He let it warm up a little before heading out from the workshop yard. The vehicle had built in satnav, amongst other gizmos, but he didn't use it much. He knew Birmingham and the surrounding suburbs like the proverbial back of his hand. He had been driving, and walking, around the area for around 40 years. He reckoned he could out fox and out drive any copper who might decide to try and pull him over. Not so easy if they got a helicopter involved of course.

Anyway, he didn't make a habit of making himself a target. He drove sensibly, within the speed limits and he kept the vehicle taxed, MOT'd and insured at all times. This wasn't the case with all the vehicles he had access to, of course. If he was using one of them, it was likely he was on some kind of covert mission. This was rare as he mainly kept the risk of his exposure to a minimum. He would get lesser members of his crew to do the risky stuff. If they got caught…tough shit. He knew they wouldn't grass him up. They would rather do some time.

As he drove through the streets of outer Birmingham, he thought back to the early days, when he and BJ had been nothing more than foot soldiers. They had been rough, tough street fighters and didn't take any shit from anyone. They had roamed the streets as a pair and had soon built up a reputation for being the ones to avoid.

This had been great for a while but soon they wanted more. More money. More power. It was all very well selling drugs on the street but the risk of getting caught was high. You might initially get a warning but you would eventually end up inside. Both Stan and BJ had been inside. That was a very unpleasant experience, although they had learned a lot from the people they had met. Some of it was useful information and contacts for when they got out of prison. Other learning was more to do with survival and how to, literally, fight your corner.

That kind of fighting was vicious...you had to react on an instinctive, visceral level, otherwise you wouldn't survive. They had both managed to survive and had come out different people. Not rehabilitated, as was the purpose of imprisonment. No, they were now harder, more determined to improve their situation. They believed, and as it turned out were correct, that by sticking together and watching each other's backs, they could succeed in their hunger and search for the power and rewards they knew were out there.

It had taken a while to get to where they were now, and if the truth be told, Stan had been the driving force behind most of the success. That wasn't to take away from the contribution made by BJ. Stan would admit that without BJ by his side, he probably would not have got as far as he had. He was, however, the one with the brains.

This worked. As a pair, they were intimidating and that was what they needed to convey on their ascent up the Organised Crime ladder. BJ might have been shorter than his nickname suggested (Big John) but he was feisty to say the least. If he wasn't too stoned, you would not want to pick a fight with him. Stan had witnessed several people make that mistake over the years. It never took BJ long to disabuse them of their initial view of him.

Stan remembered one time, quite early on, when the two of them were trying to muscle in on an existing drug dealers patch. The man had objected to their presence and had tried to intimidate them, threatening all kinds of violence, pain and even death. BJ had called his bluff and met up with him on some deserted wasteland, late one night. They had faced up, in the headlights of their respective vehicles. The man took a swing at BJ who dodged the blow, barrelled into the man, knocking him over and winding him. BJ had then proceeded to stamp on the man's head until there was so much blood his face was unrecognisable.

Stan hadn't even bothered getting out of the car. The man was dead. They had control over his area and his distributors. No one argued about it once they heard what had befallen their old boss. Shortly afterwards Stan was contacted by someone further up the line, in the misty echelons of organised crime. They were impressed and wanted to develop a long term arrangement. From then on, Stan and BJ rose quickly to a position of considerable power and wealth.

One project that hadn't worked out too well was outsourcing the growing of cannabis to willing farmers. The idea was to set up hydroponic systems in redundant barns, preferably out in the sticks. As they were agricultural premises already they would hopefully not attract the attention of the law. This was proven to be a false hope. However much they tried to disguise the operations, there were unavoidable signs that illegal growing was taking place. These included excessive electricity consumption, heat signatures over and above normal amongst others. The trend was now for renting unassuming residential properties and using them for 'urban farming'. If one property was discovered, they would move the operation on to another. The scale of each operation was such that the loss would be minor.

The cocaine side of the operation obviously relied on importing the drug. This side of things was dealt with higher up the OCG chain and on arrival to the UK, distribution was swift and widespread, using outfits such as Stan and BJ and similar throughout the country. Each of these then had thrown network of sellers to the end user.

The police would, of course, try to stamp out the use of drugs but it was a losing battle trying to arrest and punish all the users. They really wanted to find out who was controlling the system from above. The OCG bosses. These people were keen to keep out of the limelight, the drug trade being a multi-billion pound business. They were never going to give up such a lucrative income stream easily. They had no conscience so they cared not a jot for the damage the trade did to society, the deaths, both to users and dealers through drug wars.

Stan and BJ had had their fair share of confrontation with other wannabe drug barons but so far they had managed to keep the competition at bay. That's not to say they had not had any run ins with the law. They had both been to prison, having been caught dealing on the streets in the early days while they were building up the business. They both viewed this time as part of their education and a good opportunity for networking. Not quite what the law intended.

Having been driving around for while, filled the Range Rover up with fuel and bought a sandwich, Stan decided it was time to head back to base. He wasn't really achieving anything on his own. He realised he had been a bit slack and hadn't kept a personal eye on the network or dealers. He had left this up to BJ in the main. He would have to remedy this over the next few weeks. For now, though, he headed home.

CHAPTER 16

The next couple of days for Chamberlain and the team were mostly office based. Lots of takeaway coffee and buns. When he could, Chamberlain would disappear out into the carpark for a smoke of his beloved pipe. His team were working through the Neil Corrigan case files, apart from DC Dixon who was trying to do background checks on both Corrigans and the farm itself, including Rob and Susan Corrigan, the foster parents.

On this outing to the carpark, Chamberlain decided to go around the corner to the cafe, or satellite office, as he called it. A change of scene often helped the 'little grey cells' as Hercule Poirot, the Agatha Christie sleuth, would say.

He ordered a coffee and bun and went and sat at a table in the window. He liked to people watch and the pedestrian traffic past the cafe was busy today. The cafe smelled of fresh coffee, baked goods and frying bacon. It made a change from the sweaty, musty incident room from whence he had just come.

His phone pinged in his pocket. A text from DC Dixon asking where he was as she needed a word. He replied, telling her to come to his satellite office. She would know where that was and he wasn't going to waste the newly arrived coffee.

Five minutes later, DC Dixon and DS Harris arrived at the cafe. Harris must have wanted to stretch his legs and jumped at the opportunity to get out of the incident room.

"Order yourselves a drink and come and sit down" said Chamberlain.

"I'll go" said Harris. "You tell the boss what you told me" he directed Dixon.

She sat down at the little table and had a worried look on her face.

"As you know, sir, I have been trying to do background checks on all of the Corrigans. It's proved really hard and I can find little information to be honest. Robert and Susan Corrigan fostered two boys, Peter and Neil, about 22 years ago. Any previous records for the boys are sealed. I have applied for a court order but that is taking time, for some reason. Rob and Susan Corrigan had been living on the farm for many years but didn't have any children of their own, The farm was handed down from her side of the family". She paused as Harris came and sat down at the table.

"Ok, with you so far. Nothing too strange there I don't think. How old were the two boys when they were fostered?" asked Chamberlain.

"Neil was 9 and Peter was almost 15. For the

first year and a half or so, everything seemed to go smoothly. They went to the local school and helped out on the farm when they could. Then it gets weird. I can't find any more details about Rob and Susan. They just seem to disappear, although the farm bank account continues to be used, to this day. There is no record of their deaths or burials".

"Peter Corrigan did say that his foster parents were long gone. He didn't offer any further information. I should have pursued that line of questioning" Chamberlain said. He was getting a bad feeling about the whole Corrigan set up. Something was hinky.

"Should we get Peter Corrigan in for questioning, do you think Sir?" asked Harris.

"Yes, I think we should" replied Chamberlain."Organise a couple of uniforms and take Dixon with you. Bring him to the station and we'll have a chat. While you are doing that, I will pop over to see what progress they have made in autopsy".

They finished their coffee and headed out of the cafe. Harris and Dixon went round the corner back to the HQ building. Chamberlain walked over the road to the morgue where Professor Daniel Reed was dealing with the meat puzzle.

"Ah, Ralph, great timing, old boy" said Reed in greeting.

"You have made some progress then Daniel?"

queried Chamberlain.

"Oh yes, progress indeed! You know I said this was going to be really tricky, sorting out all the body parts? Well, it turns out that whoever disposed of these poor souls, inadvertently made my job a lot easier than I first thought. All the parts were wrapped in old newspapers and although there is much degradation, each body part is wrapped in newspapers with a unique date on them. I can therefore match the various body parts and make them whole again" the professor looked very pleased with himself.

"Ok, what about identification of each body?" asked Chamberlain.

"I can't work miracles, I'm afraid. Each one has been smashed in the mouth, probably when still alive, judging by the amount of blood residue, and probably with a hammer. They have also had their fingertips removed. I have sent samples for DNA testing but that will only help if they are on the system" explained Reed.

"Now for the piece de resistance! The bottom two groups of body parts were covered by a layer of various items of blood-soaked clothing. A set of male clothes and a set of female. None of the other victims had any clothing with them. The bottom couple also have no damage to their mouths or teeth. Identification should be relatively easy on those two from dental records" explained the professor.

Chamberlain thought that he probably wouldn't need an official ID for the bottom two victims. He had a very good idea who they might be. Why they were there would take a lot more working out.

"Ok, very interesting. Thanks Daniel" he said.

"Always a pleasure, dear boy" said Reed.

Chamberlain headed out of the building and set off for HQ. He had remembered the pile of old newspapers by the range in the kitchen at the Corrigan's farm. Could that be the source of newspapers to wrap the body parts, like so many joints of meat? Getting Peter Corrigan in for questioning was now even more urgent.

As he walked back across the street to police HQ, Chamberlain got his pipe out and relit what was now about half a bowl, left over from his last smoke. It meant the tobacco was a bit dry and strong tasting but it was quicker than starting again...and waste not, want not. He left a trail of smoke as he walked on.

Chamberlain loved Warwick. Such rich history. A real mix of architecture, some of which, like the Lord Leycester, dated back to Tudor times with its' distinctive wooded framing. Not much of medieval Warwick had survived the fire in1694 and much, including the current police HQ, was of Georgian design and construction. Chamberlain had his amateur architect head on as he walked up the road. He felt the local stone built buildings had a majestic quality. If only building could talk...what stories they could tell. Fantastical, he knew but what the hell. He reckoned humans didn't know everything, much as some liked to think they did.

A though occurred to him. When he retired, he could write a fantasy fiction book about how buildings retained their history and could pass it on to anyone who would listen....

He arrived at the HQ building and abruptly brought himself back down to earth. Ridiculous idea. Some of that history could be very embarrassing indeed. Some things should just be kept private... shouldn't they?

He was back in policeman mode as he made his way to the incident room and his office. He ought to spend some time in there at least.

CHAPTER 17

Judith Webster had to keep telling herself she was a journalist, a serious journalist at that. Not just some hack. Why, then, was she questioning herself? Her tutor at University had seen something in her. Professor Greenwood had encouraged her to write creatively, not just a few lines of newsprint.

Why was she finding this article so hard? Although she had felt positive after her last session and she had written lots down, she now was stumped as to how to turn it into a submittable article, not just the ramblings of a victim. Maybe because it was about herself and something that had almost cost her life. Maybe it was too soon and she wasn't fully over the ordeal. Her cups of coffee to lines written ratio was appalling. It was no good, it just wasn't flowing. She closed the lid of her laptop and sighed heavily.

Just then her mobile rang. She looked at the display and it was the letting agent that dealt with her flat. What could this be about? She always paid the rent on time. She answered the call. Five minutes later she ended the call. She was going to be homeless as the owner wanted to return to Warwick and live in the flat herself. She had a month's notice.

The day was getting better and better. Too early for wine....was it? *Fuck it* she thought to herself. She went to the fridge and as if by serendipitous chance there was three quarters of a bottle of Pinot staring right back at her.

Without further ado, she grabbed the bottle and searched out a glass from the drainer, filled it to the top and started drinking. *It's five o'clock somewhere* she persuaded herself, just like the song.

She suddenly felt very vulnerable and for some reason desperately wanted to see Ralph Chamberlain. They had only been dating a short while but he had rescued her from probable death and she was sure he would give her comfort and wise words. She would ring him....after the wine....dutch courage. Maybe some music would take her mind off things.

She had a very eclectic taste in music and her Spotify play list covered a host of genres. She set it to play random tracks and settled on the sofa with her wine. She'd brought the bottle with her and placed it on the coffee table in front of her...easy to reach and it saved having to get up to go to the fridge when she needed a top up. She took a large gulp of the cold wine and swallowed. Almost immediately she could feel the early effect of the alcohol as it went down her throat. The wine was very dry and she gave an involuntary shiver.

The first track that came on from her play list was 'Summertime' by DJ Jazzy Jeff & the Fresh Prince. She wasn't a massive Rap fan but she could hear and understand the lyrics that Will Smith was putting out and the groove was a fairly gentle soothing one. She leant back on the sofa and closed her eyes. Her thoughts went back to Ralph Chamberlain, her hero copper.

He wasn't her usual type. She wasn't quite sure what her usual type was but it wasn't Ralph Chamberlain...Detective Inspector Ralph Chamberlain, no less. She couldn't quite put her finger on why she was attracted to him. If you listed his attributes, they didn't seem like much. Medium height, neat hair, slim build, intelligent, smoked a pipe....nothing particularly dynamic, and yet...There were some little quirks, like the way he greeted you with 'Morning!' Irrespective of what time of day it was...the 'Aahh Bisto' when he took a drink. Maybe it was the little things that added up to a great package.

He had clearly not liked her, or her kind, when they had first met in her friend DCI Rebecca Flemming's office. That had changed dramatically even before their mutual adventure involving almost being killed by Neil Corrigan. The thought of that brought her crashing down and her stomach flipped.

She started to analyse the situation she found herself in. Not from a self-pitying point of view, just idly going over old memories and dreams. While Will Smith was rapping about 'Summer Madness' she remembered her University days. Carefree? Yes, to a degree...and she did get a degree! She was proud of it and had worked hard to get it, and since.

She felt sure it would be cathartic to write down her recent experience, if only she could think of the right words. She had tried to start several times but had thrown the proverbial sheet of paper in the bin every time. Another gulp of wine...it wouldn't help but it was going down so well...*like a tarts drawers* as her father used to say.

Her father. She missed him terribly. He had been a bit of a cheeky bugger and used expressions that just would not be acceptable these days. He had never meant any offence by it, it was just the era and generation he had grown up in. Locker room banter, they used to call it. Inappropriate, offensive, misogynistic language, they called it now. You had to be woke, or some such, nowadays. It used to be called political correctness.

She remembered a famous comedian once saying that it was a choice to be offended. She supposed he was right. It seemed that whilst comedians of old may have sometimes sailed very close to the edge of what was acceptable, nowadays they had to be so careful, the comedy was different, somehow. It's never right to mock the afflicted or target individuals but surely there should be no subject that can't be the object of a good joke? Judith wasn't one hundred percent sure.

She realised she had been daydreaming again and not concentrating on writing her article. Her music had continued to play in the background but she couldn't have listed what had been on. Currently, there was a Beatles track playing. One of her favourites and it had brought her out of her daydream state. 'I Saw Her Standing There' was filling the room with Lennon and McCartney harmonies. It never paled for her. It had been one of her father's favourites too. Time for more wine and to raise a glass to absent friends. Then she would start to write.

CHAPTER 18

DS Harris came storming into the incident room and headed for Chamberlains office. His boss was sat there, deep in thought.

"He's gone" said Harris, breathlessly.

"What? Who's gone? Where?" Said Chamberlain, not yet realising what Harris was telling him.

"Corrigan....gone!" said Harris.

"Are you sure? He has a big farm. He could be anywhere on the 300 acres or he could just be out" Chamberlain tried to rationalise.

"Nope, definitely gone, sir. When we got there, some bloke was loading up a bunch of cattle into a transporter. Apparently he bought them off Corrigan for a really good price, cash. Same with the machinery in the yard, which, by the way, included a mini digger and an old tractor with lifting forks attached. Apparently Corrigan told him he had had enough of farming and was going travelling" blurted Harris.

"He's got the wind up after we saw him the

other day, asking about the farm and his foster parents. I think it's them at the bottom of the freezer and I think he killed them" said Chamberlain.

"I'll get out an All Ports, he might try and leave the country by the sound of things" said Harris.

"We need to catch the bugger and question him. If he is another serial killer, he needs to be stopped. At the least, he has covered up potentially what his cousin Neil has done but I think it is more than that" Chamberlain paused. "Could there be two serial killers in the same family?" He was asking himself more than anything.

Chamberlain got up and walked across the incident room. He needed to brief DCI Flemming. As he left he called back to Harris.

"See if you can find a picture of Peter Corrigan and get it circulated" then as an afterthought "and get Dixon and Norrish down to that pub and see if Peter Corrigan ever drank in there with his cousin" and then before he got far down the corridor he came back and shouted " and get Bewley and his SOCOs up to the farmhouse and go over it with a fine toothed comb".

He knocked on Flemming's door but didn't wait for a response, just walking straight in.

"Well, do come in" said his boss, sarcastically.

"Peter Corrigan has done a runner and I think he is also a killer" Chamberlain blurted out.

"Jesus, are you sure?" she said in surprise.

Chamberlain brought her up to date with all they had discovered, including the body parts in the freezer and the dates of the newspapers, and the fact that the victims appeared to be of Afro Caribbean origin, culminating in their conversation with Corrigan and the subsequent discovery of him selling the cows and machinery.

DCI Flemming looked back at him, a very serious look on her face. Something was obviously troubling her.

"Ralph, I have a horrible feeling I have misjudged a situation. You remember that solicitor, Frank Williams, who came in the other day?"

"Yes, the one I was supposed to talk to. I did apologise for that" said Chamberlain.

"Yes, yes, it's not that. He told me that his client was worried that a number of his operatives had disappeared over the last few years and he had been tasked to go round the local police forces asking if any unidentified bodies had turned up" explained Flemming. She waited for this to sink in.

"Fuck! You think the bodies in the freezer might be his client's operatives?" said Chamberlain.

"It's got to be a possibility. I am pretty sure these clients of Williams's are an OCG from

Birmingham, probably Yardies, and certainly involved in drug distribution. Why would Corrigan be killing them?" said Flemming.

"The only way we are going to find out is by asking him" said Chamberlain.

When he got back to the incident room, he found Dixon and Norrish taking off their coats having just got back from their visit to the Bell and Tankard pub. He wanted to hear what they had found out.

"How did you get on at the pub then?" he asked.

"Quite interesting actually sir" said Norrish. "We spoke to the young barmaid who recognised the picture of Peter Corrigan. She said she had seen him a couple of times, firstly with his cousin Neil, a few weeks ago, and more recently a couple of days ago, He was asking people if they wanted to buy his livestock and machinery"

"He also approached one of the younger lads in the pub asking where he could get some drugs" said Dixon. "This lad thought it was weird as he didn't specify what sort of drugs, as if he had never done it before".

"Did he tell him where he could get some?" asked Chamberlain.

"No. He thought he might be an undercover cop so steered well clear" she replied.

The drug trade seemed to be rife, all over the UK. Some would argue that the government were missing out on massive amounts of tax revenue by not legalising cannabis. Many states in the USA had already taken this path. Opponents would argue that cannabis was a gateway to harder, more harmful drugs like cocaine and heroin.

Chamberlain was fully aware of the wide use of these drugs, not just by the traditionally viewed hippy, layabout types. Many professionals and ordinary working people partook of cocaine. He even suspected some of the officers he came across in the police force of using cocaine to keep awake and enthused by the job. Uniform branches were very often finding drivers under the influence of these drugs. They seemed to think that if they weren't drink-driving then anything else was ok. You didn't just get breathalysed these days, they most likely would do a mouth swab for drugs as well.

The distribution of such popular merchandise was everywhere, including in pubs and clubs. Licensees had a duty, by law, to keep an eye out for, and report, any drug dealing on their premises. Penalties were severe and could include losing their premises licence.

"Ok, that sounds odd. Do we think Corrigan is clearing out? Or changing direction with the farm or simply giving up farming and just living in the farmhouse?" Chamberlain was asking himself these questions as much as his team.

"Trying to sell for cash in a pub sounds like desperation to me" suggested Norrish.

"Agreed" said Dixon "You're not going to get a good price and people are going to be suspicious and suspect the stuff is knocked off".

"Ok, see if you can find out if he advertised anywhere else. I hear what you say but very often pubs are where business is conducted, particularly among rural and farming communities, so I wouldn't make too many assumptions" Chamberlain said.

"I'll check out livestock and agri machinery sales and auctions Sir" volunteered Dixon.

"Excellent. Who's turn is it to fetch up the coffee and buns then?" Chamberlain was a big fan of feeding the troops and keeping them awake with regular caffeine hits.

"I'll go" said Norrish.

"Good lad" said Chamberlain. His DC was shaping up well "Here's some dosh. Go to the cafe rather than the canteen, please". The coffee was much better and the buns....they were so much better than the cardboard tasting ones from the canteen.

Norrish returned about fifteen minutes later, laden with the required provender. He was getting quite adept at carrying multiple cups of hot drink together with paper bags full of buns. What skills he was picking up as a murder detective.

When they were all settled with their snack, Chamberlain re0started the conversation.

"Ok, what do we think about the pub landlord and Verity...and the pub as a whole?" he asked the room.

"All seems fairly innocuous" said Harris "Rob Jones and Verity have been very cooperative...maybe a little too much so but I may be being unfair on that score".

"I agree. Let's file that for another day and when we have time we can speak to uniform and get them to keep an eye on it. Licensing issues are not really in our remit, certainly not while we have a psychopathic murderer on the loose" said Chamberlain. He swigged down the last of his coffee and wished the cups were bigger. The bun was enough to keep him going but more caffeine would not have gone amiss. He didn't really have time to go out for a smoke either.

Neither Dixon nor Norrish mentioned their suspicions about what went on in the toilets at the pub. That was for another day, maybe.

CHAPTER 19

Peter Corrigan was a little put out, to say the least. That bloody policeman, Chamberlain, was getting too close for comfort. Maybe his cousin Neil had been right to target him. Shame he hadn't succeeded.

Corrigan was now virtually homeless and all he had was a bundle of cash and his pick up truck. He didn't want to go back to the farmhouse. He was going to continue to try and find the bosses behind the drug gang, if it was the last thing he did.

He was getting good at recognising dealers in the street. They had a certain way about them. Previously they had usually worked solo and had been easy to pick off, one by one. None of them had given him any useful information however. At least they would no longer pedal their poisons.

Now, however, they seemed to be working in pairs. This was new. He wasn't sure he could safely take on two at once, although he was a pretty sturdy man, a farmer, used to physical work. Two on one changed the dynamic considerably. So he had missed a few opportunities recently.

He was currently driving around the suburbs

of Birmingham, looking for what would probably be his last chance. Once last piece of scum off the streets. If possible, he would extract the information he needed but if not then no one could say he hadn't tried his best to avenge the death of his foster parents. It wasn't that he had particularly loved them, or even liked them. It was the effrontery, the inconvenience, the shit that he and Neil had had to go through to protect their lifestyle and stay at the farm. Someone should pay.

Then he saw him. A lone figure, loitering under a lamp post. Typical skinny black youth, hoody pulled up over his head, looking down at his phone, occasionally looking up furtively. Yes he was definitely one of them. He would watch him for a while, just to make sure. See him make a deal, a sale.

He parked the pick up at the side of the road. He was about 75 yards away from the lad. It was a safe distance. His only worry was that by now the police were probably looking for him, and his truck. It was impossible to disguise the vehicle.

Just then, a shiny black 4x4 drove slowly down the road past him and stopped side the youth. The windows were darkened so he couldn't see the occupants. He had a sudden flash back to that day his foster parents had been killed. The black 4x4 he had seen driving away. It couldn't be the same one. This one had last year's number plate registration but it was the same style of pretentious vehicle. Maybe this was the bosses. At last!

It was a Range Rover Vogue. The driver was

clearly speaking to the lad, and the conversation appeared animated. The youth got into the back seat of the vehicle which then pulled away. Corrigan followed. This was more like it.

Meanwhile, inside the Range Rover, Stan Hemmings was tearing a strip off the young lad, who was cowering in the back.

“Wah di fuck yuh doing out here pan yuh own?” Stan shouted at the terrified youth.

“Sorry boss but mi reckoned mi did safe here” he proclaimed.

“Yuh nuh fi tink, yuh nuh pay tuh tink” Stan was furious. He had made it clear that none of the crew were to go out on the streets on their own. “Stupid madafucka”.

Stan was so inflamed that he didn’t notice the pick up truck following him. He drove around at random for a while and then made a decision. He would find another distributor and drop this lad off with him and hope that they followed orders and stuck together. If only he had know he had just saved this lads life, yet in the process, put his own life at risk.

Eventually they saw another dodgy looking character outside a fish and chip shop. The lad in the car confirmed he was one of theirs so Stan dropped him off.

“Yuh bloody well stick togetha, right?” He told the boy as he got out of the car.

"Yea boss" came the reply.

Stan drove off leaving the two lads, complaining together that they didn't like working in pairs but they were more frightened of Stan than they were of anything else so they would comply.

A pick up truck pulled out from a little distance behind Stan and continued to follow him. The two lads left behind were unimportant now. Corrigan was fairly sure the man driving the Range Rover was the big fish he had been looking for, for so long. He had some very searching questions to ask this man. If it turned out that he was involved all those years ago in the death of Robert and Susan Corrigan, then he was in big trouble. If not, he may have information about who was. Either way, his fate was sealed as far as Peter Corrigan was concerned.

The target in front of him seemed to be driving around the suburbs of Birmingham without any sense of direction. A couple times other vehicles would pull out in front of Corrigan and he nearly lost sight of the Range Rover. However, it was a very distinctive vehicle, shiny black, dark windows and big, low profile tyres. He soon caught sight of them again and caught up.

He realised he was sweating now and he could hear his heart beat, thumping against his chest. He so didn't want to fuck this up, having spent years searching…and killing.

CHAPTER 20

Ralph and Judith had met for coffee, in the 'satellite' office. She had suggested they meet and there were things they needed to discuss. He had agreed. He leant across the table and took her hand. She had soft skin and delicate fingers.

"So, I guess we have both seen the enormous elephant in the room since the Corrigan ordeal" said Ralph.

"I guess" said Judith, hesitantly. She knew what she wanted to talk about but she had no idea what he had on his mind.

"Rebecca reckons I should talk to someone....you know, like a therapist. I'm not sure I want, or even need to" he said. "How about you?"

"Well, I don't know really. I suppose the article I am trying to write is, or I hope it to be, my therapy. And that's mainly what I wanted to ask you about" she said. She wasn't ready to tell him she had already had a few sessions with a therapist.

"Ok, ask away" he wasn't sure how he could help. He wasn't really creative in a writing sense, not like her.

"I am having trouble starting the article at all. What's hanging over me is what happened between you and me. The rescue by the hero policeman and the relationship that seems to be developing" she explained.

"What about it?" he asked nervously.

"Well, it's a major part of the story but I don't know how much of it to include in the article. I don't want to compromise your career or anything like that" she said.

"Ah, I see. I hadn't really thought about it from that point of view. I don't see that it matters from my side. I was doing my job. I mean, I know I killed someone....I took a life, and that's quite a heavy deal and something I will no doubt have to reckon with but as I say, I was doing my job. Have you spoken to Rebecca about it?" he asked.

"Yeah, briefly. She said to talk to you about it" Judith smiled.

"Well from my point of view, you can write what you like, as long as you make me out to be a James Bond style hero and that you couldn't help falling in love with me....." he stopped, realising he had used the 'love' word without thinking.

Neither of them said a word for several moments. They just sat there and looked at each other across the table, her hand still in his. Rather than withdrawing her hand, she squeezed his and smiled again. *Phew* he thought. Maybe he hadn't overstepped the mark then.

"Well, obviously" she said at last. He wasn't sure whether she meant the James Bond thing or the mention of love. He decided not to pursue the question. She had visibly relaxed.

"Thank you Ralph, I think I will be able to at least make a start on it now. What did you need to talk about?" she enquired.

"Err…well…actually, I think we just covered it. I hadn't talked about the fact that I killed Neil Corrigan, a sort of denial maybe, but now I have mentioned it, I don't feel such a weight on me about it. Was there something else on your mind? You said 'mainly' when I asked you earlier what you wanted to discuss" he said.

"Ah yeah. I'm going to be homeless very soon" she just came out with it. "My landlord wants to move back to Warwick and has just given me a months notice".

"Oh, shit, what are you going to do?" Even as he said it, he had an idea, which might be crazy and she might think it ridiculous.

"I don't know. Start looking for another flat I guess. It's a pain in the arse and the timing is spectacular. I feel safe where I am. I am not sure how i would cope with moving into somewhere new" she looked downcast again. He hated seeing her like that. He smiled at her.

"I have an idea. You may think it crazy but it might help us both out. Don't dismiss it without giving it some thought, please" he said.

"I'm intrigued" she said, leaning forward.

"Why don't you come and have a proper look at my basement flat. I haven't done anything since I lost Mrs Frobisher and I think it would suit you perfectly. I know, I know....a bit weird me being your landlord and your boyfriend but we would deal with that, I'm sure" said Ralph, enthusiastically.

"I was more thinking about the fact that I would be moving into the flat of a kidnapped and murdered woman" said Judith, looking a little worried.

"I understand that. But she wasn't killed in the flat" he wasn't sure how else to reassure her.

She leaned back and thought for a few moments. He just kept hold of her hand and hoped she would come round to thinking it was a great idea.

"You'd have to let me have my own space and not keep sneaking into my bedroom without asking" she said.

"Absolutely. You would never see me" he said

categorically.

"Don't be a twat. I would want to see you...a lot. But the flat would have to be my space. I need some privacy" she explained.

"Yeah, yeah...that's what I meant" he said.

"I'll think about it" she said, simply. Inside her head she was conflicted. It would be fantastically easy just to say yes. It would be the answer to her problem. However, was she ready to get that close to this man?

They let that hang in the air and talked about other things for a while as they finished their coffee. She was keen to get started on her article now that the weight had been lifted and he needed to get on with finding Peter Corrigan.

CHAPTER 21

Peter Corrigan was hot on the tail of the Range Rover... his long time target, as far as he was concerned. He would, of course, ask the man nicely if he had murdered his foster parents all those years ago. He was planning the questioning as he drove along behind the black Range Rover.

A couple times he thought the driver had spotted the fact he was being followed but he didn't do anything about it. He just kept driving back in the direction of the north side suburbs. Corrigan followed him turn off the A4540 and head into the Nechells area. He was unfamiliar with this part of Birmingham and became somewhat disorientated.

The Nechells suburb of Birmingham is situated North-East of the city centre, has historically been an area settled by immigrants and has a diverse population. Despite their sense of community the area is ravaged by poverty and residents here feel neglected by the authorities. It has a reputation for criminal activity, in particular, drug dealing.

Soon, Hemmings turned into a small industrial estate. At the end of one of the roads, which appeared to be a dead end, Hemmings turned into what looked like a scrap yard, with wrecks of cars dotted around, interspersed with a few that looked as if they might be roadworthy with a lot of luck and a fair wind behind them.

Corrigan stayed back a little distance and watched as Hemmings parked his vehicle next to a roller shutter door in the grotty looking building. His heart was pounding in his chest and he was sweating slightly. He cracked the window a little to let in some air. He received what was the unmistakeable aroma of a sewage works. He shut the window again.

Hemmings raised the roller shutter, rather than going in through the open side door, having removed a sturdy looking padlock. Corrigan could see a little way in to the workshop. There was a hydraulic ramp, partly raised, with what looked like an old Rover perched on it.

A side door, probably an office, owned and another man came out, looking half asleep and dishevelled. He had what looked like a very large cigarette hanging out of his mouth. Even though he was much older than he had been back then, Corrigan recognised him as the passenger he had seen in the black 4x4 leaving the farm all those years ago.

Gotcha, ya bastard thought Corrigan to himself. He continued watching for a while. With two men in the workshop he wasn't so confident. He just had to hope one of them would leave at some point.

His wish was granted about 20 minutes later when the driver walked out of the workshop and headed out of the yard, walked straight past Corrigan in his car and headed up the road. He didn't notice the man sat in his car as his head was down, looking at his phone.

Now was his chance so Corrigan waited until the man was out of sight and got out of his car and walked slowly towards the workshop. Out of the corner of his eye he spotted something half hidden in the corner of the yard. He looked over and say the rusty remains of a very sad looking Land Rover Discovery. It was black.

Again his memory flashed back 20 years. He was that teenager again, watching that black 4x4 drive away from the carnage he was about to discover in the kitchen of the farmhouse that was his home. His anger flared and he walked into the workshop. He saw the dreadlock man in the office, with his back to him. He calmed himself and called out to the man.

"Hello there?" he called.

The man jumped slightly and turned around to face him.

"Yea wah yuh wa" said BJ.

"Err, I am looking for some parts for my car" said Corrigan, innocently enough.

"Wi too busy, cum back next week" said BJ, rather abruptly.

"But I see you have an old Discovery out there which matches the year of mine and might have the right parts on it. To be honest, I'd buy the whole thing probably" enticed Corrigan.

"Di boss isn't here an yuh wudda tuh aks him" came the reply.

Corrigan was struggling a bit with the Patois but he persevered.

"When will he be back? I can wait" he said.

The man looked half asleep and was not being very helpful. The cigarette he was smoking was giving off a peculiar aroma. After a few moments of thought the man appeared to come to a decision.

"Mi wi ring him an aks"

He turned away from Corrigan and picked up his phone, dialling, presumably, his boss. Corrigan couldn't make out the conversation but there was a lot of nodding. He spotted a lump hammer on the bench next to where he was standing, picked it up and moved closer to the man on the phone who still had his back to him.

BJ ended the call, put his phone back down on the desk and was about to turn around. He didn't make it, instead slumping to the floor, dead. Corrigan had struck him a hefty blow with the hammer on the back of his head.

One down thought Corrigan. He left the man where he had fallen, blood starting to pool around him, leaking from the gaping wound in the back of his head. Even in death, the joint was still in his mouth, smouldering. Corrigan just stood, staring down at him for a while. Then, having wiped the handle, he put the hammer back down where he had found it and walked back out of the workshop, to his car, to wait for the return of the other man. He didn't have long to wait. He could see the man walking back down the road towards where he was parked. Just before the man reached him, he got out of the car and hailed him.

"Hello there. Your mate said I should speak to you about one of the vehicles in your yard that I am interested in" said Corrigan.

The man stared at him, trying to sum him up. He looked a lot more with it than the other man had. Corrigan would have to be more careful here. The man simply nodded towards the workshop and carried on walking, assuming Corrigan would follow him.

"Which cyar yuh taking about?" asked Stan.

"The old black Discovery over there, in the corner" answered Corrigan.

"Nuh wuk, dat un" said Stan.

"Oh, I am only interested in it for parts but I would take the whole thing off you for the right price" said Corrigan.

Stan just shrugged and indicated for him to follow him to the office. He presumably thought he was going to negotiate a price but as he drew near the office, he saw BJ lying on the floor.

"Wah di fu...." He didn't finish the expletive as a blow struck him on the side of his head. He wobbled a bit and sunk to his knees. Corrigan hadn't hit him as hard as the other man. He wanted a chat with this one, but not here. He applied a little chloroform on a cloth and the man went into a deep sleep. That had been one thing his little cousin Neil had been useful for, the chloroform.

Corrigan had already decided that he liked the look of this man's Range Rover. Much more comfortable than his pick up, and it would confuse the coppers if he was in a different vehicle, at least long enough for him to get where he wanted to be to spend some quality time with his guest. He gathered some tools together from the workshop as he had left his own at the farmhouse. He then loaded the unconscious man, whom he had cable tied and gaffer taped, into the back seat of the range rover, extracted the keys from his pocket, climbed in and drove away. All very neat, he thought.

He headed south, back the way they had come, as he knew no other way to go, until he recognised where he was. He could now head towards home, though not actually go to the farmhouse. No, he was headed straight for the Copse.

CHAPTER 22

Chamberlain was sitting in his DCIs office again. He was briefing her about the latest that had come up from Pathology and Forensics. They had confirmed the identities of Robert and Susan Corrigan from official Fostering Service records. There was also evidence from the autopsy that they had both been stabbed multiple times in what must have been a vicious attack. Although they had been dismembered, it appeared to have been done with more care than all of the other bodies. Whoever had done it had just cut off the arms and legs, neatly, wrapped all the bits up in newspaper and placed them in the bottom of the freezer, finally covering them with items of their own clothing.

The other bodies were not yet identified. They had been cut up into smaller pieces with less care but also wrapped in newspaper. All they had been able to garner from the remains was that they were all afro Caribbean and aged between late teens and early twenties. Mostly male but one female amongst them.

They would probably eventually be able to estimate at least the month and year of death for each of them, partly due to the state of decomposition and partly the dates on the newspapers. Full IDs may come later if they were on the system and they could match DNA.

"Jesus, what a sick mess!" said DCI Flemming when here DI had finished the briefing. "And what the fuck....two psychos in one family?"

"I know, hard to believe, though they are not related by blood as far as we know" said Chamberlain. "I've also just heard from the SOCOs up at the Farmhouse. Richard Bewley and his team have gone over the whole place and come up with some interesting stuff".

"We need more information....we need a break... so what have they got?" asked Flemming.

"Richard says I need to go up there, which I'll do as soon as I can" said Chamberlain.

They needed to warn Frank Williams, the OCG Solicitor, urgently that his client may be in danger from a marauding psychopath with a vigilante attitude to drug dealers. They wouldn't quite phrase it like that, of course.

"Call Williams in, Ralph, and we can have a serious chat with him" said Flemming.

"Yup, will do" he replied. "I've asked Judith to move into my basement flat" he blurted out. She probably knew already but he wanted to know what she thought of the idea. She did know as Judith had rung her.

"Yes, I know" she said, raising her eyebrows higher than Chamberlain thought possible.

"Don't give me that look, and don't say it" he could imagine she was seeing wedding bells and all the trimmings.

"I wouldn't dream of saying anything" she said, innocently.

"And don't even think it" he snapped.

"Ah, too late on that front, my friend" she said "I hope you'll both be very happy. Now bugger off and get on to that solicitor".

Chamberlain left her office, the colour rising in his cheeks. He wanted to say 'Shut ya face' to her, but he felt he had already used up any goodwill there might have been between them when he rushed headlong into a dangerous situation without proper back up. He knew he had been lucky.

He went back to his office and put a call out to the solicitor's office. Frank Williams said he would come down straight away. He had nothing on today. Chamberlain reckoned he probably didn't have many, if any, other clients apart from the OCG that he was retained by.

To pass the time while he was waiting for the man to arrive, Chamberlain took a stroll outside with his pipe. He sat on the retaining wall of the car park and looked around him. He loved the architecture of

Warwick, mixed as it was. There were traces of Tudor timber framed buildings but most of them had been destroyed by fire. Many had been replaced by Georgian stone built buildings.

At one time he had thought he would like to be an architect....his phone pinged. The solicitor had arrived. He must have parked elsewhere and walked through the front door to the building as Chamberlain hadn't seen him arrive. He knocked the embers out of his pipe on the edge of the wall, stood up, and made his way back into the HQ and to the meeting room where he was told that Frank Williams was waiting for him.

"Mr Williams" he said on entering the room."I'm Detective Inspector Chamberlain. Thank you for coming in so promptly"

"Well, your DCI said it was quite urgent, so here I am. Do you have any news for my client?" he asked. He appeared rather nervous. Chamberlain wasn't sure whether it was his presence or the nature of any news he may have to relay to his client.

"Possibly" said Chamberlain. "We have made some discoveries and the nature of these leads us to suspect that your client may be in serious and imminent danger"

Frank Williams looked as if he might cry. Chamberlain didn't want to give all their cards away so he didn't go into the full, horrific, details of their discoveries.

"Suffice to say, we need you to contact your client and warn him, or them, and give us their name and address so we can arrange protection as soon as possible" said Chamberlain.

"Oh I don't think Sta....my client is going to like that very much, Inspector" almost saying the name of his client. It was enough for Chamberlain.

"It's Stan Hemmings, isn't it" he had thought it might be but this confirmed it for him.

"I never said that" said Williams, defensively.

"Don't worry, we know Stan very well. I even helped put him away for one of his stints at Her Majesty's Pleasure....oops. I suppose it is now *His* Majesty's Pleasure isn't it" Chamberlain corrected himself.

The solicitor was looking more and more distraught. Chamberlain could imagine the threats Hemmings would have made to this man to get him to keep the confidentiality of client/lawyer privilege.

"Just ring him and give me an address" said Chamberlain as forcefully as he could. "I'll go out of the room and give you some privacy" He left the room.

Pacing up and down the corridor, he would have given a lot to be able to hear both sides of the conversation going on in the room. However, he was surprised to see the solicitor come out of the room.

"I can't get hold of him. I have tried a few numbers but there is no reply" he looked worried.

"Is that usual?" asked Chamberlain.

"No, not at all. I can always get him on one of his numbers"

Chamberlain knew it was common for this kind of criminal to have several contact numbers. He had a hollow feeling in his gut about this.

"Give me the address....NOW" he shouted at the cowering man.

Frank Williams wrote down the name and address of his client and passed it to Chamberlain who ran from the room and up to the incident room.

"Listen up! We have an emergency. I believe Peter Corrigan is going after this man, Stan Hemmings, for reasons I will need to confirm, but we need to move now. Harris, with me. We are going back to the farm. Dixon and Norrish, get hold of the local plod nearest to this address and get them to check it out, very carefully. Warn them about Corrigan." Chamberlain was barking orders left right and centre.

"I'll just go and brief Flemming" he said and rushed off to her office.

There was a slight pause and then pandemonium as everyone got on with their tasks.

Chamberlain met Harris in the car park and they drove off, at speed, with Chamberlain at the wheel. They followed the familiar route out to the Old Birmingham Road and on towards the Farm House that Corrigan appeared to have abandoned.

When they arrived, there were several vehicles parked up and a hive of activity. They got out of the car and sought out Richard Bewley. They found him supervising the extraction of various items from the property to be loaded into one of their SOCO vans.

"Ah, about time. Get suited and booted please. There is much to see but we haven't finished by a long chalk so I don't want any contamination" said Bewley. He was clearly under pressure and in no mood for any frivolous remarks, which was unlike him.

Chamberlain and Harris did as they were told. When they were ready, Bewley indicated for them to follow him. They went in to the farmhouse through the front door and he led them immediately into the living room.

"This is obviously the living room" said Bewley. "I want you to see this first as it is probably the crux of the whole case".

They followed him over to the side wall of the living room where there was a very large mirror hanging on the wall from a chord that was fixed to a hook on the picture rail above. Bewley lifter the mirror away from the wall and reversed it on its' hanging.

There, on the back of the mirror, was what could only be described as an incident board. The first impression Chamberlain got was that some of the material, notably at the top, was very much older than that further down. In the middle at the top were two rather faded photographs. One of a man, the other a woman. They were fixed to the mirror using sellotape which had aged and looked like it would peel off at any minute. Underneath was written 'Rob & Susan - killed 5th April 2002'. Underneath these were two other smaller photographs of two young boys and writer underneath was simply the words 'Neil age 11' and 'Peter age 16'.

These photographs were clearly the oldest things on the board. Underneath were some random sentences about a black 4x4 probably a Land Rover. There was a newspaper article stuck to the mirror, again using sellotape but not as old. It appeared to be about a farmer in Suffolk growing cannabis in a barn. It referred to a possible gang connection to the Birmingham area.

Harris had started taking photos of the board, first in its' entirety, then individual aspects of it. Chamberlain was just staring at the board, his mind working overtime trying to work out what it all meant. As he moved his gaze further down the board there were lines drawn down to boxes drawn in some kind of marker pen. Each was numbered, from 1 though to 7. Each box had some writing in it, of varying amounts. Chamberlain found the words hard to distinguish. There were also a couple of empty boxes.

Seven boxes, seven bodies in the freezer, apart from Rob and Susan Corrigan. Chamberlain began to form a theory but he needed to know what the writing in the boxes meant before he could confirm it.

"Richard, have you been able to decipher the writing in the boxes? I am having trouble making it out" he asked the CSI.

"Yes, it's tricky isn't it. A scrawling hand... rather like a Doctor's notes. The easy bit is that each appears to have a date in the top left hand corner. These start about 10 years after the date next to the top two pictures, and not long after the date of the newspaper article, and work their way almost to the present day. This seems to be a systematic journey of discovery, prompted by the article" replied Bewely.

"Anything else?" asked Chamberlain.

"Only the odd word or two is immediately decipherable. For example, in this box I can see the words 'nothing known' and in this one 'might be connected' but full analysis will be needed to get the full text I'm afraid" replied Bewely.

"Ok, thanks Richard" Chamberlain was conscious of time pressure. He wanted to get out and about, looking for Corrigan. "Anything else you need to show me right now?"

"Oh, there is plenty to show you but if you are in a hurry then just one other thing for the moment"

Bewley could tell Chamberlain was itching to leave.

Bewley led them out of the room and through to the kitchen. On the table was a mid sized leather holdall. Next to it were laid out a number of implements. These included a couple of claw hammers, a saw, a bunch of cable ties and a pair of pliers. A tool kit, of sorts.

“This bag was found underneath the sink behind some old paint tins” explained Bewley.

“A bag of old tools” said Chamberlain.

“Yes, very astute, Inspector Clouseau” said Bewley, sarcastically referring to the bumbling French detective played by Peter Sellers in the Pink Panther films.

“Ok, explain” Chamberlain was getting more frustrated and looked at his watch.

“So impatient” muttered Bewley. “We did preliminary tests on the tools and they have been crudely cleaned but still show traces of blood. We will have to confirm if it is human blood but I would suggest we both know the answer to that”.

“His kill kit” Chamberlain said.

“Kill, and possibly torture, I might venture” said the CSI.

“Christ. We need to catch this wacko” Chamberlain said to Harris. “We need to go, unless there is anything else you need to show us Richard?"

"That will do for now. The rest can probably wait for my preliminary report which should be with you sometime tomorrow" answered the CSI.

CHAPTER 23

Chamberlain and Harris were just pulling away from the farmhouse when the radio came to life with a message for them.

"Go ahead control" acknowledged Harris.

"Message from local officers at the addresses given for Stan Hemmings. No one was at the home address. Different story at the workshop. They discovered a body, as yet unidentified. Rather messy apparently. Head smashed in with a lump hammer" said the voice from control. "It's not Hemmings though. No sign of him or his vehicle but there is a pick up parked in the road outside, registered to a Peter Corrigan, again, of whom there is no sign".

"CCTV, Harris" shouted Chamberlain.

"Control, can you check to see if there is any CCTV at the workshop" said Harris.

"That's a negative, they already checked"

"Ok, received control" Harris said, finishing the call.

"They must have gone off in a different vehicle. I'm not surprised there is no CCTV. If Hemmings is what we think he is then he wouldn't want the comings and goings there, being recorded. How the hell are we going to find them now? They could be anywhere" said Chamberlain.

"We can find out what vehicle, or vehicles, are registered to this Stan Hemmings, through the DVLA. I'll put the call in" said Harris.

"Check under the business name as well" added Chamberlain.

Harris got on to the task while Chamberlain continued driving. He wasn't sure where to head but it beat not going anywhere. His head was spinning with all the information from the farm and now this from the Hemmings place. He had a theory but he wasn't confident enough to air it yet.

He thought it through again. Peter Corrigan kills his foster parents, for whatever reason, possibly with the help of Neil but that was unlikely as he would have only been 10 or 11 at that time. He might have helped his older cousin with the disposal. That would probably be enough, combined with his early childhood, to set him on the path to full serial killer.

Peter Corrigan gets a taste for killing and find easy victims in young black drug dealers. Easy to find and very few questions asked when they disappear. Could it be as easy as that?

But then, what about the newspaper article on the board describing the Suffolk Farmer and the cannabis growing? Then he had a thought.

Harris had finished his call and was waiting for information to come back to him.

"Tom, what if Peter Corrigan didn't murder his foster parents?"

"What are you getting at Sir?" asked Harris.

"What if someone else murdered them and this has all been about revenge?" said Chamberlain.

"Ok, but then why did he bury them and not report the murder?" Harris was thinking aloud.

"Hmmm" was the only response he got. They drove on in silence for quite a while.

Harris's phone went. He took the call, made acknowledging grunts for a while and then hung up.

"Right. The business has a couple of vehicles registered to it. A tow truck and a flat bed truck. Stan Hemmings has a private registration for a Black Range Rover Vogue" he relayed to Chamberlain.

"Check with those local officers but I suspect they will be in the Range Rover and not either of the trucks" said Chamberlain. "Get it out to the ANPR centre and see if we get any hits on it".

Fancy black 4x4. A business address in the Nechells area of Birmingham. Sounded like drug dealers to Chamberlain. OCG bosses liked to show off. Power play. Big egos. Chamberlain's theory was starting to grow legs and if not fully running, at least hobbling along.

CHAPTER 24

Stan started to come round. His head hurt and his limbs were restricted. He was very uncomfortable. There was some kind of tape over his mouth so the fruity language he wanted to direct at his captor came out as a load of muffled grunts. He soon realised he was lying across the back seats of his own vehicle, his beloved Range Rover Vogue, his symbol of power. Well he had no power at the moment. The irony was lost on him.

He could see the back of Corrigan's head as he concentrated on driving the vehicle. Stan had no idea where they were or where they were going. This must be some kind of gang takeover bid but why hadn't the guy just killed him and had done with it? He struggled against his restraints, to no avail.

Corrigan must have noticed and half turned his head towards Stan while keeping an eye on the road.

"Well, well, morning sunshine" he said. "I've spent years trying to find out who you are and tracking you down. I have to say, your oppos were all very loyal to you. None of them gave me any significant information about how to find you. You may have noticed some missing over the years. Yes, that was down to me!"

Stan wriggled with fury. So this was the guy 'disappearing' his crew. If he could get free he would show him. But he couldn't get free. He was trussed up like a jerk chicken.

"Anyway, we will have a proper chat when we get somewhere more private" said Corrigan. Stan didn't like the sound of that, at all. He couldn't get the sight of his old friend BJ, lying, he presumed dead, on the floor of his office at the workshop. He was a waster but he was Stan's oldest friend, confidante and business partner. There was a lot of blood and his head didn't seem right.

"This is a great car to drive, by the way" said Corrigan to his prisoner.

If the mumblings could have been heard properly they would have sounded like…

"Fuck off yuh mada fucking bastard. Mi a guh fucking kill yuh"

"No, sorry, didn't catch any of that" mocked Corrigan.

He drove on, at the same time enjoying the driving experience but also worried that any minute he would be spotted and the chase would be on. Nothing happened. He was free to navigate his way back to the Old Birmingham Road and travel south towards his destination.

He was loving the comfort and performance of the vehicle. Some nerd could probably tell him in detail but all he cared about was the obvious power produced by what he assumed was a diesel engine. The leather seats were comfortable and there were loads of buttons to play with, not least a superb sound system. When he turned it on there was obviously some Jamaican reggae programmed in. After fiddling about a bit he found a classical station. He turned up the volume so as to drown out the mumblings and groaning of the man on the back seat.

It was almost with regret that he soon saw the familiar features of the land either side of the road which meant he was nearing his own land and access to the copse where he intended to interview the man in the back. He realised he hadn't even confirmed his name yet. Time enough.

CHAPTER 25

Judith Webster was making her way to Ralph Chamberlain's house. He had given her a key so that she could go and have a look at the basement flat, in her own time, when she felt ready to do so. She had been curious, rather than ready. Curious about the flat and curious about how she would feel being in that space, knowing what she did about the previous occupant and how they had died.

She hadn't known Mrs Frobisher so there was no personal connection. Even so, she needs to know she could do this. It did make sense in so many ways, for her and for Ralph.

She parked her car in the street outside the house. She had been there before of course but never down into the basement flat. She had keys to both entrances and decided to go in through the flat front door. She went down the steps and opened the door. There was a slight musty smell as she entered. The place needed airing. She decided to leave the front door open, partly for this but also to quell the feeling of claustrophobia that was welling up in her.

The flat still had all Mrs Frobisher's stuff in it. Ralph had warned her of this so it wasn't a surprise.

It still felt a bit weird though. Calming herself she started to look around. The rooms were a good size, matching those above in the house. She tried to imagine what it would be like without the rather dowdy furnishings of the previous occupant.

Yes, this could work she thought.

The hardest room to look in was the bedroom. Here there were the personal trappings of a woman, the hair brush and make up on the dressing table, the flowery bed linen on the bed, a glass of water still on the bedside table.

Judith decided that was enough for now. She went to the hall and found the internal stairs that led to the upper floors...Ralph's domain. She had been there before of course but her focus had been on the man himself, not on the house. She would have a sneaky look round now. He wouldn't mind, would he?

As she got to the top of the stairs she noticed a different smell which she recognised as residual pipe tobacco smoke. It wasn't wholly unpleasant to be honest. In the lounge she noticed a large bookcase along one wall. She went over to peruse the titles of the books. There seemed to be quite a lot about architecture and also travel books. Some of the tomes were modern but there were also quite a few old, leather bound volumes. She ran her fingers along the spines of the books, trying to relate this to the man she had fallen for.

And yes, she had fallen for him big time. If

you had asked her to describe her perfect man, Ralph Chamberlain would not have come close. Just goes to show how wrong we can be about what we actually want.

She turned to the room and looked across at the fire place and the mantel above it. There it was. Warwick bloody Castle. The scene of her near death and heroic rescue by DI Chamberlain. The rather beautiful painting of the castle made her shiver. She was not sure she would be able to keep looking at that day after day.

She walked across the room towards the painting. She stood in front of it for some while trying to dispel the feelings of fear and hatred welling up in her mind. She couldn't. In a sudden fit of outrage she reached up and lifted the picture off its' hanging and went to put it against the wall so that she could no longer see the castle. As she went to turn away she noticed an envelope tucked into the frame on the rear of the painting.

She got an urge of curiosity and pulled the envelope free. It clearly contained something. On the front it simply had the words *DI Chamberlain.* It wasn't sealed, rather the lip was simply folded into the envelope. Her curiosity grew and grew. She eased it open and took out the paper from within. She shouldn't be doing this should she. But she did.

She unfolded the paper which appeared to be some kind of letter. Scanning to the bottom, there was a signature. A name. She became light headed and sank to her knees. There on the sheet was the name

Neil Corrigan.

Her breathing became fast and her hands were shaking. What the fuck was this doing here? Did Ralph know about this? Questions kept coming into her head. Was there some kind of conspiracy between Ralph and Corrigan? No, she was being ridiculous now, her mind playing tricks on her. She wondered if she had the courage to read the letter or should she give it to Ralph first?

Neil Corrigan was dead. He couldn't hurt her or Ralph anymore but he was still there, from beyond the grave, so to speak. She made her decision. She would ring Ralph and tell him about it and see what he suggested they do with it.

CHAPTER 26

Peter Corrigan had turned off the main road, oblivious to his pursuers, and had made his way deep into the Forestry Commission pine wood. He had decided not to go straight to the copse. He would deal with the man in the back in the usual place and then take him to the copse to dispose of him. This was, he hoped, the boss man so he might be difficult to crack. It could take some time.

Being a managed forest, there were plenty of rough tracks that crisscrossed the area, none of which were a challenge for the 4x4. He found his usual, little used track and turned into the darkness of the forest canopy.

When he thought he was far enough into the forest he stopped the Range Rover and sat for a while. The mutterings and what he assumed had been cursing, had subsided. All these years of looking and he finally had the chance to draw things to an end. Closure. It didn't feel as good as he had thought it would. It was now just a job that had to be done.

He opened his window slightly. The sweet smell of pine and the fading light were somewhat soporific. He closed his eyes and drifted for a while.

He realised how tired he was. He could take 40 winks, surely? It would be better to wait until dark to do what he planned in any case. He eased into that sleep but not sleep kind of state, aware of where he was but semi-conscious. He half dreamt about when he and Neil had been boys, playing on the farm. Then he was at the farmhouse looking in at the horror scene that he had discovered in the kitchen. He woke with a start. Time to get on.

He got out of the vehicle and opened the rear passenger door. A pair of bound feet made a feeble attempt to kick him.

"Whoa there, sunshine" he mocked his prisoner "this ain't my first rodeo, you know. Let's get you out of the car and put you somewhere more uncomfortable".

Corrigan felt a little more clear headed after his little doze. He dragged the man out of the car and along the ground for about 30 feet, then sat him up against a tree, then passed a rope around Hemmings's neck and the tree. Not too tight. He wasn't finished with the man yet, just wanted to keep him upright and still.

"I think what I will do is explain to you what is going to happen now, and what information I need to hear from you. That way you will know what to expect and we might get done here in quick time. How does that sound?" he said. He knew he would get no reply at this stage as the man still had gaffer tape over his mouth. The eyes, however, said it all. They were burning with anger. He would soon change that. Fear. That was what he needed to infill in the man. So to work.

"First of all, my name is Peter Corrigan. Does that name ring any bells with you? Either nod or shake your head" he instructed the man. He shook his head.

"Ok, a bit of history then, about 20 years ago myself and my young cousin Neil were living relatively happily with our foster parents on a farm, not far from here. I was 16 art the time and my cousin, 11. One day, we came back from playing out on the farm only to find that Rob and Susan...our foster parents...had been stabbed to death in the farm kitchen" Corrigan looked at the man's eyes to see if there was any recognition yet. Still the anger shone out.

"Right then. In a minute, I am going to remove the tape from your mouth and I am going to ask you some questions. You will answer, truthfully, or I will hurt you. Simple as that".

He went to the rear of the car and retrieved the small selection of tools he had taken from the man's workshop. He laid them on the ground in front of the man, for effect.

"Yes, I am going to use some, or all of these. They are your tools. Somewhat fitting, don't you think, that they should be the instruments of our entertainment?". He went over to the man and removed his shoes, tossing them in the back of the car. He went back and removed the tape from his mouth, slowly and painfully, he hoped.

"Firstly, what is your name?" said Corrigan.

"Fuck yuh, yuh fucking cunt" said Hemmings.

"Oh dear, is that the best you can do?" asked Corrigan. "Looks like it is going to be a long night. Don't get me wrong, I will enjoy it. You....not so much".

If anything, the anger, the fury, shone brighter in the man's eyes.

"Well, I know your name now anyway. Documents in the glove compartment. Mr. Stanley Hemmings"

"Yuh nah get away wid dis" groaned Hemmings.

"Well, whether I do or don't doesn't really concern you to be fair. Now, stop wasting time. Did you and your dead friend there, back at your workshop, kill my foster parents 20 years ago?"

There was silence. Corrigan picked up the pliers and with one swift movement, crunched one of Hemmings's toes between the jaws and squeezed tight. Hemmings screamed with the pain.

"Shh, shh now, you'll wake the squirrels" said Corrigan, releasing the pliers.

He was pretty confident that they were far enough into the forest for no one to hear the screams but still, poor wildlife.

"Right, you have nine other toes to work through, and then of course there are the hands and if necessary, the more intimate parts of your body. Do you want to reconsider my question?" Corrigan asked calmly.

Stan Hemmings considered himself a tough man and reckoned he could put up with quite a lot of this treatment. Maybe this man would give up after a while, maybe not. The police must be looking for them by now having discovered BJ's body. He was sad and furious that this man had killed his friend. How could he avenge his death? He needed to buy some time and work out an escape plan.

"Mi need sum wata. Den mi wi tell yuh everything" he said gruffly.

Corrigan thought about this for a moment. The man was probably dehydrated and would last longer if he did give him some water. The problem was he didn't have any to hand. He was also quite hungry himself as he hadn't eaten since that morning. He came to a decision.

"Ok, fair enough. I will go and get some

supplies. It could be a long night and we will both need sustenance. If you are trying to trick me I will be very unhappy and you will feel the consequences" he said to his captive.

He tightened the rope slightly and checked the other restraints. Once satisfied he went to get in the car.

"You be good now, don't go anywhere" were his parting words. He reckoned he could get to a late night garage and back within half an hour or so. Once in the car he started it up and drove off.

CHAPTER 27

Judith dialled Ralph's number and waited for him pick up.

"DI Chamberlain's phone" said a voice she was unfamiliar with.

"Ralph?" she queried.

"No, this is DS Harris. The Inspector is driving. Who's calling please?"

"It's Judith Webster. I need to talk to him urgently" she said. She sounded distressed so Harris handed the phone to his boss.

"You'd better take this sir" he said.

Chamberlain was driving along a fairly straight piece of road with little traffic so he took the phone from Harris.

"Hello?" he said.

"Ralph...it's Judith. I need to see you. I found something at your house. It's a letter from Neil Corrigan. You need to see it" she was speaking at 90 miles an hour.

"Whoa, slow down Judith, what are you talking about?" he said. She sounded very flustered which was unlike her. He became immediately concerned.

"Corrigan! He must have been in here. He left a letter for you tucked in the back of the frame of that painting of Warwick Castle" she explained to him.

"What does it say?" he asked. At the back of his mind he was wondering how she had found it but that could wait.

"I haven't read it, Ralph. I can't" she was almost in tears.

"Judith, listen to me. Take the letter and go to the HQ and find Rebecca. I will meet you there, ok?" said Chamberlain.

"Ok" came the reply, and she rung off.

"Shit! We have to go back to HQ" Chamberlain said to Harris. He explained the nature of the brief phone call and then sped up, heading back to the centre of Warwick. Their search for Peter Corrigan would have to wait for the time being. He couldn't believe that Neil Corrigan was still getting at him... and through Judith as well. The poor girl must be going out of her mind.

When they finally got back to the HQ, Judith was already there, sitting in DCI Flemming's office, cradling a hot mug of coffee. When she saw Ralph, she leapt up, spilling the coffee on her hand but she didn't notice She had clearly been crying. She put the mug down and rushed over to him, throwing her arms around his shoulders. She couldn't help but burst out crying again.

"Hey, it's ok, I'm here" he said, trying to calm her. "Where's this letter?".

"I've got it here" said his boss.

Chamberlain guided Judith back over to her chair and turned to Flemming, reaching out for the letter. He took it and started reading it immediately. There was silence in the room for quite some time as he digested the contents. It read, as follows:

Dear Detective Inspector Chamberlain,

If I don't win my little game, you may, or may not, find this note. If I am in prison now, or dead, you should know a few things about me and my so called cousin Peter.

It may be that you are dead, in which case it doesn't matter. Someone may not find this for decades.

My cousin and I were fostered from different backgrounds. We never really discussed each others' history. When Peter was 16 and I was 11 our foster parents were brutally murdered, by whom, we did not know. We didn't want to give up our lives on the farm so we hid Robert and Susan in a chest freezer.

Eventually the smell became so bad that we had to bury the freezer in the woods. After that we spent a few years fraudulently making it look like the farm was running as per usual. Pretty clever that. Once Peter was 18 it became easier. We hired in cheap labour when we needed it. It was a pretty steep learning curve but we managed it.

When I got old enough I decided I wanted to get out into the world. I had urges. Urges I couldn't satisfy on the farm. I went out and got myself a job and a little place to live. This is about the time when we almost first met and what led us to where we are now.

Peter had been mighty pissed off with whoever had killed our foster parents. I wasn't so bothered to be honest and I thought we had done pretty well with the farm life. However, something changed about 10 years after their death. Peter saw a newspaper article about a farmer in Suffolk who got caught growing cannabis in a barn. He said he just rented the barn out to some businessmen from Birmingham and didn't know what they were doing.

I didn't know how this was relevant at the time but from then on Peter would go out for long days, returning very late into the night, sometimes early morning.

When I returned to the farm after a spell sleeping on the streets (your fault) I questioned Peter about it. I insisted he tell me everything.

It turned out that our foster parents had been killed by a drug gang who were pissed off that Rob & Susan would not agree to grow cannabis in one of the barns. For fear they would tell the police about it, this gang killed them. Peter has been hunting them down ever since.

So there you have it, our tragic little story.

Your Humble Servant

Neil Corrigan

P.S. feel free to send a copy of this to the press.

Corrigan blew out a huge sigh and sat down in a chair next to Judith. He looked from one to the other women in the office. He didn't really know what to say. He had known, or at least suspected, that Neil Corrigan had been in his house, which was why he had chosen the castle for their ordeal. He had no idea that he had left a letter for him. It was creepy. No wonder Judith had been so spooked.

"Judith, I'm so sorry it was you who found this, and on your own. It does kind of confirm what I was thinking though. I originally thought one of the Corrigans had killed Robert and Susan, most likely Peter as Neil would have been very young at the time of their death. This confirms otherwise. Peter has been on a long term vendetta because someone else killed them" said Chamberlain.

They all sat there in silence for a while, lost in their own thoughts. The quiet was broken by the sound of the desk phone ringing out loud and clear. It had clearly made Judith jump. DCI Flemming answered the call.

"Yes, speaking. Right, go ahead......Ok......

where?" she queried. The call ended.

"Stan Hemmings's vehicle has been clocked by the ANPR system on the main road coming out of the South side of Birmingham. It looks like it is heading down the Old Birmingham Road" she relayed to the other two in the office.

"What? But that's heading right back towards the Corrigan Farm. Surely he would know it is going to be crawling with Police?" suggested Chamberlain.

"Well, at this point we don't know he is heading there. He could have another destination. We need another sighting to confirm his whereabouts" said Flemming.

"I need to head out there and help the search. Will you be ok here Judith? Stay with Rebecca". She nodded. She wasn't going anywhere.

"And Ma'm, can we get the helicopter up to join the search, preferably before all the action is over!"

The last time they had needed air cover, when Neil Corrigan had kidnapped Judith, they had arrived on scene just after DS Harris had pulled his boss out of the River Avon. He had tumbled over the battlements of the castle with Neil under him in a desperate act to rescue Judith. Chamberlain had survived but the psychopath had not had time to take a breath as the policeman's charge had winded him. He had drowned.

"I'll get on to them now. You get off and don't

worry about Judith, she is safe here with me" said Fleming.

Chamberlain gave Judith a hug and a quick kiss and left the room. He summoned Harris and went off to the car park. As they were getting into the car, the radio crackled into life.

"You take it Tom" said Chamberlain. He was busy strapping in and getting the car going.

"DS Harris receiving, go ahead" said Harris.

"Another sighting of target vehicle by a mobile ANPR van on the Old Birmingham Road" came the message.

"Do you have a location" asked Harris.

"Vehicle has just gone under the M40 flyover, travelling down the A3400. Speed approximately 60 miles per hour" said the dispatcher.

"Ok, keep us updated. Over and out" said Harris.

Chamberlain had heard the conversation. Corrigan wasn't in any hurry by the sounds of things. Trying not to draw attention to himself maybe. If they were quick, maybe they could get to the farm before him, if that was where he was headed.

He sped out of the car park and immediately found himself in heavy traffic. Blues and twos it was then. In his experience, most people would do their best to get out of the way of any emergency services vehicle that was flashing and sounding sirens. However, in close traffic, it only took one plonker to just sit there for it to make their efforts to speed up the process of getting through traffic to be ineffective.

Chamberlain found himself behind one such vehicle.

“For fuck’s sake” he swore loudly. “Move!!!”

Nothing happened. Then, after a few agonising moments the vehicle indicated left. Not because of the impatient policeman behind him but because that was where he wanted to go. He was in no rush to complete the manoeuvre either.

“In your own time, you.....” Chamberlain couldn’t decide what form of insult to use so he just tightened his lips and waited for the road to be clear.

“Please let me have occasion to pull you over one day matey” he said as they passed by the offending vehicle. He accelerated, then slowed for the next queue of traffic.

“This is ridiculous” said Chamberlain.

“Take the next left, sir. I know a back way that should avoid this traffic” said Harris, who was sitting nervously in the passenger seat. An annoyed DI Chamberlain was not a pleasant experience in a car.

“I don’t know why we bother with the blues

and twos, I really don't" moaned Chamberlain. The traditional UK siren was a two-tone "nee-naw" siren which has mostly been replaced now with American-style wail, yelp or phaser sirens. The original two-tone sound was created by two different horns operated alternately. New sirens use one speaker, or two playing the same sound.

Chamberlain felt the pressure of his pipe against his leg. It was in his trouser pocket, as usual. What he would give to be able to light up at this moment. He would have to wait.

He took the next left as per Harris's guidance. He said to take the second right and that would take them parallel to the main road. He was right, there was little traffic.

"This comes out at a roundabout that joins back onto the main road, Sir" said Harris.

It did, and they had missed a long queue of traffic. They were now back on the main road they needed, to get to the area where the farm was located. They didn't know for sure whether Corrigan was going to the farm but they should be able to intercept him whatever his destination. With police cars trying to catch up with from behind him and maybe the helicopter on the look out for him soon, he shouldn't be able to get away.

They rushed along towards the Old Birmingham Road, no need for the Blues and Twos now. They made good progress and were soon approaching the lay-by that gave access to the hidden path that led through the woods to the scene of the recent murders and discovery of the bodies in the freezer. This time they were not stopping here, nor did they take the track that led up around the back of the woods to give access to the path from the other side.

They drove on, watching out for a black Range Rover which should be coming from the opposite direction. After another 5 miles or so Chamberlain began to think something was wrong. There was no sign of the target vehicle. Then Chamberlain's heart sank as he saw a number of police vehicles rush by on the other side of the road. Corrigan had given them all the slip. How the hell had that happened?

"Shit, where the hell is he?" said chamberlain.

"He must have turned off somewhere" said Harris, who then got on the radio and relayed the message to control and the other police vehicles.

"Find out the exact location of the last ANPR hit and we will got as far as that and then work our way back" instructed Chamberlain.

Harris made the enquiry. "The last hit was the mobile unit that was parked under the M40 flyover" he told Chamberlain.

Chamberlain increased his speed. He wanted to find this man as soon as possible. It was likely that he had Stan Hemmings as a captive and his life would be in serious peril.

"Can you phone DCI Flemming and bring her up to date and whilst you are at it, ask how Judith is please" Chamberlain was worried about her, though he knew her friend Rebecca would look after her. After the call, Harris informed him that she was fine and was sleeping in one of the meeting rooms. The DCI wanted to be kept updated direct.

Chamberlain was fully aware of the irony of chasing one criminal in order to save another. It was his job, Hemmings may have broken the law but as a policeman, Chamberlain couldn't just let Corrigan's vendetta take its' course, however justified it might be.

"And I want regular patrols up and down the A3400 in case he shows up again" said Chamberlain. He continued up the road until he got to the flyover and he did a somewhat illegal U-turn, at some speed. Harris gripped the armrest even tighter. Once they were safely heading back down the main road, Harris sent the message through regarding patrols.

A much and as hard as they looked on the journey back down the Old Birmingham Road, they could see no sigh of the black Range Rover. There were a myriad of turnings that he could have taken off the main road but it would take forever to search each one.

The helicopter, now on scene, was having no better luck in the search and would soon have to return to base to refuel.

"Damn it, where is this man? I am getting fed up with chasing psychopaths all over the place" said a very frustrated Chamberlain. They would have to return to base and leave the patrols to keep an eye out for Corrigan. Chamberlain wasn't holding his breath on that front.

When they got back to the Police HQ in Warwick, Chamberlain went straight to his DCI's office in search of Judith. She was not there. He panicked, until Flemming told him she was asleep in one of the meeting rooms.

"Before you go to her Ralph, just remember what she has been through. She is a strong woman but it was one hell of a shock for her when she found that letter. She might not admit it but it set her back a bit, I could tell" said Flemming.

CHAPTER 28

Back in the pine forest, Stan Hemmings was trying to thinking fast. His head was still a little fuzzy from the blow to his head and the dose of chloroform. He had to try to escape this madman who had already killed BJ. He had no idea where he was but it was clearly a pine forest. He could smell the sap and feel the fallen pine needles between his toes.

His toes. The one that his captor had savaged, was throbbingly painful. It made it hard to concentrate. *Think!* The rope around his neck, although not very tight, was rubbing, making it sore. The whole restraint system made it very difficult to wriggle in order to try to get free. Stan was surprised the man hadn't gagged him again. He could shout for help. Fuck the squirrels.

"Help" he shouted as loud as he could, into the darkness, only trees to hear him. There was no response.

He was really thirsty. It wasn't particularly cold, and thank god it wasn't raining. The ground was a little damp but that was the least of his problems. The sounds that a forest makes at night can be very disconcerting. It wasn't an environment that Stan was familiar with. He was a townie, really. The night time sounds of the city held no threat for him but amongst the trees, in the dark, he was a little nervous.

Every little noise seemed to be amplified by the darkness. The situation in which he found himself didn't help his demeanour either. He chastised himself. How could he have been so careless and let this guy get the drop on him. He wriggled against his restraints again but they were too tight and it hurt to move too much. What was he going to do? If only he had chosen to arm himself that day....but then, who was he kidding. He turned his back on a stranger and having a gun in his belt would have made no difference.

An owl hooted, up in the trees, some distance away. Stan wasn't sure he had ever heard an owl in real life. Then he heard what sounded like a baby screaming at first. Then he realised it was a fox calling out in the night. Shit...would a fox come up and have a go at him? Surely not. He was getting paranoid and fantastical now, probably due to the dehydration and hunger. He also felt sick, his head hurt and he needed a piss. He had no choice, he would have to wet himself. No doubt his captor would have some acerbic comment to make about that when he returned. He let his muscles relax and felt the warm liquid fill his trousers. It was temporary relief from the cold as soon his damp clothing made him even colder. He could feel the heat dissipating through the steam rising from his groin.

A loud crack broke the silence of the forest. Stan jolted, resulting in pain from pretty much all over his body. Being a city boy, he was unaware of the sounds of the trees as branches fell off and hit other branches before hitting the forest floor. There was nobody there but his imagination started seeing shadows. He shouted at the darkness.

"Who di fuck dat?"

Nothing in response.

"Eff yuh playing tricks pan mi...." It was an idle threat as he was powerless to do anything to anyone.

"Fuck, fuck, fuck" he screamed helplessly.

In some ways he wasn't too surprised by his situation and he probably deserved it to a degree but he wasn't finished yet. This wasn't the way he wanted to go out. The image of his old friend BJ lying dead on the floor of the office in the workshop came to him again and a tear made its' way down one cheek.

He tried again to free himself, pulling as hard as he could against the rope and cable ties. The pain was excruciating and he passed out.

Nighttime noises returned to the forest as Stan sat unconscious, crumpled against the tree. An owl hooted and its' mate responded, both hunting their prey. A fox was brave enough to slink past the recumbent figure, within ten feet of the tree, sniffing suspiciously as it went, also hunting for a night meal but not liking the odours emanating from Hemmings.

It moved swiftly away into the darkness of the trees.

When Stan came round again, he had no idea how long he had been out, The forest was still black as night. There was an eery silence. No more hunting animals rustling through the undergrowth or swooping through the trees. A great shiver went through Stan's body. He had no more strength to fight against his bonds. He would have to try and make his move when his actor returned...if he ever returned. Maybe he was just going to leave him out here to die, on his own. The way he was feeling, that probably wouldn't take too long. What a way to go out. No blaze of glory. No final showdown. Just left to rot in this stinking forest.

His mind was starting to play tricks on him. He thought he heard BJ telling him to hang on.

"Yuh chrang mi bredren. Help wi cum" said the voice in his head.

"Thanks BJ but mi nuh tink help wi cum" Stan said to no one but the darkness.

CHAPTER 29

DC Dixon and DC Norrish had been busy doing background checks and processing the evidence that the CSIs had found at the Corrigan farmhouse. Most of it was what you would expect from a working farm. With no women living there, and no sign that they had anyone come in to clean, the place had been pretty grimy. It was just a fact that, on the whole, men and women had different priorities in terms of keeping a house and that applied particularly to a farm house. The nature of the work and the hours spent doing it, didn't leave much time for cleaning.

It was late and dark outside but being a CID detective meant you didn't do strict office hours. You worked for as long as it took to get the job done. It took copious amounts of coffee, take-away sandwiches and sticky buns. Occasionally someone would bring in a pizza or two. They were having to put up with the canteen coffee as the cafe, or satellite office, around the corner was closed.

Richard Bewley, the lead CSI, had produced a preliminary report. Dixon was still getting used to reading this kind of report as she was the newcomer with less experience than others on the team. She had to start somewhere so Norrish had left her to it.

"How are you getting on with that report" he asked her.

"Not too bad, thanks. Once you get used to the lingo, it all starts to make more sense" she was trying to convince herself as much as Norrish.

"Anything stand out at this stage?" He knew he was being unfair but would relent before long. He was teasing her really.

"Well actually, yes. They found quite few pairs of boots, as you would expect on a farm. None of them clean, in fact most had a significant amount of mud on them" she looked at Norrish, knowing he would pick her up on her findings. She let him have his moment.

"Well, not very surprising for a farm, don't you think?"

"Absolutely....only there is a different kind of mud on one pair of boots. Most of them have mud which is common to the farm and surrounding woodland. The odd dead, deciduous leaf stuck within the mud. This one pair has pine needles lodged in with the mud. They haven't found any pine trees around the farm as yet" she explained.

Norrish perked up his interest. This was actually potentially useful information. He was embarrassed to have been slightly mocking of her efforts. The truth was, he fancied her and was trying his best to avoid those kind of feelings. This manifested itself by him treating her dismissively. He wasn't proud of it but he was pretty sure that his boss would not approve of that kind of fraternisation among his team. In any case, she had a boyfriend, by all accounts.

"Let's get one of the uniforms to research the area and find out if there are any woods with pine trees" he said. He set this in motion. It may be nothing but then he always remembered his boss's mantra of paying attention to every detail.

The writing and language expert guy they asked to look at the back of that mirror has come back to us with what he reckons it all says" said Dixon.

"Ok, can we get the original photos and the translations up on the screen, side by side?" asked Norrish.

Dixon took a few minutes to organise this and then they spent some time looking at the results. They fairly quickly decided that it was a rather sinister and macabre record of a series of killings but with the intention of finding out information that would lead the killer to a certain person or persons for some reason.

There had also been found some interesting paperwork. An old cheque from a joint account with both signatures of the two dead foster parents. A sheet of paper with the signatures clearly copied time and again. Someone had obviously been practicing forging these signatures. There was also an old scruffy notebook with what appeared to be a series of usernames and passwords listed in it.

"This stuff would go some way to explaining how they managed to live here on their own after the foster parents were killed" said Norrish.

"I'll go and update the boss" said Dixon, meaning her immediate boss DI Chamberlain. She was also going to use the opportunity to raise the question of her colleague's behaviour towards her. She didn't want to be a sneak but it was bugging her. She found Chamberlain in his satellite office, the cafe round the corner. This was good as there would not be any nosy buggers to hear the conversation.

She updated her boss with what they had found and he seemed impressed so she took a breath and decided to broach the other subjection her mind.

"Sir...Im doing ok, aren't I? I mean, I know I'm fairly new but you, at least, seem happy with my work" she said.

Chamberlain sat up and took a sip of the coffee he had been nursing. From the way she had phrased her question he detected some doubt in her abilities, perhaps prompted by someone else's feedback.

"Dixon, I am very pleased with your progress. Yes, you have stuff to learn but that doesn't come overnight. At this stage, I am more interested in your enthusiasm and keenness for the job. You seem to have that in spades so don't worry yourself. Why do you ask?" he queried.

She hesitated for a moment, not sure if she wanted to continue. She bucked up the courage and went for it.

"It's Norrish sir. He always seems to be putting me down and not valuing my ideas and so on" she said.

"Ahhh" Chamberlain thought for a moment as how best to phrase his reply.

"The thing is, Dixon, us men are essentially simple beings. The stereotype cliche of beer, sex and football is usually pretty accurate, though not necessarily in that order. When it comes to you ladies, a confident or arrogant man will simply chase you until you hopefully give in. A more sensitive man may be very shy when it comes to the opposite sex and may resort to insults or dismissive comments as a form of self-preservation to counter a fear of rejection. What sort of man do you think DC Norrish to be?"

"What?...are you saying what I think you are saying, sir?" said Dixon.

"Do I have to spell it out for you Dixon?" said Chamberlain.

"Err no, I think I get the gist" Dixon flushed pink and wished she was anywhere else but where she was right then.

“Are his comments derogatory in any way? Because if so, that is a different matter and I would need to have a word” said Chamberlain.

“No, not really…” said Dixon, as if in a bit of a trance.

Chamberlain told her to keep an eye on it and to let him know if things developed in a nasty way. Then he thought about his team and the different stages of life they were all in, including himself. Life did follow certain patterns however unique individuals thought themselves to be. He chuckled and decided to go out for a smoke.

While out in the car park, his thoughts continued about himself and Judith. He had been dismissive when his boss, DCI Flemming, had told him about her, judging her on her occupation rather than actually meeting her. Another of his least favourite sayings was ‘don’t judge a book by its’ cover’ . Everybody did, it was inevitable. It was having the courage to open the book even if the cover was initially disagreeable…he suddenly wondered when he had become such an expert at relationship advice. He certainly couldn’t be accused of applying such advice to himself.

CHAPTER 30

Peter Corrigan had driven to the first Service Station he could find, on the main road. He didn't need fuel as his captive had kindly filled up recently, by the looks of it. He went straight into the shop and picked up a basket. As he wandered around he thought to himself what a limited choice there was. Not to worry. Just some sustenance to get through the night.

He put two 1 litre bottles of water in the basket and two ready made sandwiches. As an afterthought he added a couple of bars of chocolate. Treats. He then went up to the till and paid. The cashier loaded a plastic shopping bag for him. Idly, he thought, that was rare. They usually made you fill your own bags these days.

He hadn't noticed the marked police car pull into the forecourt of the service station. By the time he saw it, he was out of the door. They had clearly spotted him and the Range Rover. It was blocked in. There appeared to be no escape. He walked cooly past the police car and put his shopping in the rear load space. Then he went round to the front and got in the driver's door.

He was about to start the vehicle when it was

suddenly surrounded by uniformed police officers, all shouting at him to get out of the vehicle and down on the ground. He held his hands up and did as he was bid. Two or three officers pounced on him and pulled his arms behind his back, cuffing his hands together.

He was then unceremoniously dragged to his feet and almost thrown into the back of the police car. Two other cars had arrived in the meantime, lights flashing. It seemed a little excessive to Peter Corrigan. He hadn't resisted. The officers were barking into their radios. They seemed very excited. He heard his own name and then another that he recognised. Detective Chamberlain.

As the police car pulled away, he noticed other officers frantically searching the now abandoned Range Rover. All they would find would be his shopping. In some ways, Corrigan found the whole process rather amusing. Inconvenient at this point, for sure, but the frantic police officers were a bit like the keystone cops in those old black and white silent movies, rushing around in their inimitable slapstick fashion.

As they drove away from the service station, Corrigan wondered how Stan Hemmings would fare on his own in the forest. He didn't want him dead yet, so he hoped Hemmings would survive until they let him go. He was confident they would let him go as there was no evidence against him, or at least only circumstantial evidence.

The car he was in had its' lights and sirens on still, as they rushed along the road towards Warwick.

Corrigan knew they were passing the entrance to the pine forest that he had used and where his captive was hidden. He didn't look at it as they passed. He didn't want to give anything away.

They arrived at the police HQ in Warwick and he was bundled into the building and then what he assumed was an interview room. He sat in the chair provided and waited. And waited. He wasn't sure how long it was but time was definitely passing.

———

DI Chamberlain had been in his office when there came a shout across the incident room.

"They've got him. They've got Corrigan!" It was DC Norrish who had taken the message passed up to CID. A cheer went up in the room. Although possibly not terribly appropriate, it was a release of the tension that had been building for some time now.

"Right. We'll let him stew for a bit and then I think we should have a little chat with Peter Corrigan" said Chamberlain.

He hadn't had a chance yet to go and see Judith but maybe he should let her carry on sleeping. If she woke, she would go back to Rebecca and she could get in touch with him.

He went outside and retrieved his beloved pipe from his pocket. The filling of the bowl with the Capstan Navy Cut tobacco was a much a ritual as part of the smoking process. He would remove a few flakes from the tin and tease them out in his hand. Then he would form a rough ball and put it in the bowl of the pipe. Next, tamp it down with a knuckle, put the pipe in his mouth, light a match, put it to the tobacco and start puffing. In a few moments there would appear a cloud of pipe smoke with its' distinctive smell. He enjoyed the process for a few minutes and walked around the car park as he did so.

Time for a word with their guest.

Corrigan had waved his right to a solicitor. Chamberlain and Harris were sat opposite him in the interview room. They had completed the formalities and cautions.

"I'll get straight to the point, Peter. Where is Adio Johnson, AKA Stan Hemmings?" asked Chamberlain.

"Whose that, now" said Corrigan, innocently.

"Stan Hemmings, the owner of the garage you went to earlier today, and also the car you were caught in" said Chamberlain.

"Oh, the black fellow?" said Corrigan.

"Yes" Chamberlain realised this man was going to play games.

"No idea, Inspector" Corrigan said.

You were at his garage workshop today and now you have his vehicle. How do you explain that?"

Chamberlain was pretty sure he couldn't.

"Indeed I was, and yes I do. It's a wonderful vehicle, you should try it. The black man said I could test drive it as long as I left my vehicle as security, which I did, as you no doubt are aware. You will have found it at this man's garage" Corrigan was confident he could talk his way out of this.

Chamberlain was non-plussed for a moment or two. He was not expecting this. A different approach was needed.

"We did find your vehicle, Mr Corrigan. We also found the body of a man who had had his head smashed in. What can you tell us about that?"

"Gosh, that's awful but I know nothing about it I'm afraid. There was another man in the workshop when I was there. Dreadlocks, very stoned. Is that the chap?"

"Very dead, now" said Chamberlain. "How do you explain that?"

"Well, I can't really but if I had to guess…maybe something to do with drugs? They are always killing each other aren't they? Drug wars, they call them I believe".

Chamberlain ignored that one. "So why that vehicle? Why that garage? Do you often go to the Nechells area? I wouldn't have thought it was your scene really Peter"

"A fortunate happenstance, Inspector. I took a wrong turn and was going to ask for directions when I saw the Range Rover just sitting there in their yard. So I went in and enquired" replied Corrigan.

In an attempt to catch him off guard, Chamberlain said "We found your foster parents by the way. At the bottom of a buried freezer in the woods on your land"

"Oh, that's sad. Neil really was a bad boy, wasn't he?" Corrigan hadn't missed a beat.

Very neat thought Chamberlain to himself. Blame the dead cousin for everything.

"From forensics and other evidence, it would appear they have been dead some 20 years. If Neil had killed them, he would have been only about 11 years old" Chamberlain suggested.

"Well, they do start young these days. They grow up so quickly, don't they?" Corrigan's flippancy was not lost on the detective.

Chamberlain could see that this wasn't going to be easy. They would have to get some irrefutable evidence that Peter Corrigan had been involved with the death at the workshop and the disappearance of Stan Hemmings.

"Ok, we will leave it there for the moment. I need to speak to a colleague but I will be back in about half an hour". Chamberlain got up and left the room, Harris close on his heels. When they were far enough away Harris spoke.

"You didn't mention the letter that was found at your place, Sir"

"No, not yet. I wanted to keep something back" explained Chamberlain.

Back in the incident room, Chamberlain called the team together and brought them up to date and stressed that if they couldn't get a break, Corrigan might walk out of the building a free man. When he had finished, he asked the room if there were any updates for him from the checks they had been doing from forensics.

"I've been trying to get a history of the Corrigans, Rob & Susan" said DC Dixon. "They inherited the farm from his parents back in the 70s. They were both quite young and newly married. They worked the farm and kept themselves to themselves. Working all the time I guess. They had no children naturally but fostered Neil & Peter when they were getting on a bit. They had no one to pass the farm to so probably thought they should do something about that"

"What about the two boys? Any history there?" asked Harris.

"The Fostering Service are sending over a file for Neil Corrigan as he is deceased. They can't for Peter as he is still alive. They would need his permission. The woman I spoke to was able to tell me that Neil's upbringing was pretty brutal. More details when I get the file" replied Dixon

"Ok, anything from forensics? They must have been all over that farm by now, and of course, they have Corrigan's pick up now as well" asked Chamberlain.

It was Norrish's turn to report.

"Yes, sir. They have found traces of blood in the back of the pick up, They are doing tests to confirm whether animal or human. Being a farm vehicle it could just be animal blood. He also reported on the findings from the farm including the mud and the pine needles.

"Interesting. Ok, thank you all. Keep at it. We need to nail this man" said Chamberlain.

Chamberlain went back to the interview room. He was determined to crack this 'looney killer'. He sat down opposite Peter Corrigan again and looked at his demeanour. His face was expressionless. To all intents and purposes he looked like a normal human being, a farmer. Chamberlain had to prove otherwise. If, as he suspected, this man had kidnapped Stan Hemmings, what had he done with him. Why hadn't he killed him at the workshop like the other man.

"So, Peter. Where is Stan Hemmings?" A simple, direct question to start off with.

"I've told you Inspector, I have no idea. Why would I?" Corrigan answered simply.

"We found a bag of shopping in the back of the Range Rover with two sandwiches and two large bottles of water. Who are they for?"

"All for me. I was, and still am, hungry" said Corrigan.

"And the water? Surely you have running water at home, if that is where you were going?" Chamberlain wanted to put some pressure on the man.

"Yes, indeed, we do. But I prefer bottled water for drinking. The farm gets its' water from a well and sometimes it can taste a bit funny" Corrigan seemed to have an answer for everything.

"I suggest you have got Hemmings prisoner somewhere, for some reason, and need to feed and water him. I also suggest that you killed the man at the workshop but not Hemmings as you want him alive for the time being. What can you tell me about that, Peter?" Chamberlain asked.

"Well, it makes a good story but I have no idea what you are talking about" Corrigan was still calm, though sounded a little frustrated.

"Your pick up, that you abandoned at the workshop. They have found traces of blood in the load area at the back" It was a statement, rather than a question. "We are waiting to find out if it is human blood but I think we both know the answer to that, don't we?"

"Firstly, I didn't abandon the pick up, as you well know. I left it there as security while I test drove the Range Rover. Regarding my pick up. It is a farm vehicle so is likely to have animal blood in it. If it is human blood then we are back to Neil's exploits. We shared the vehicle" Corrigan answered smoothly.

"Tell me more about what happened to your foster parents, Rob and Susan. You said before that they were long gone. What did you mean by that?" Another change of direction in an attempt to catch the man out.

"You'd have to ask Neil about that, but then, you can't now, can you" he was getting smug now, thought Chamberlain.

"Interesting you should mention Neil actually. We found a letter that your cousin had secreted in my house. It was a confession to everything. The relevant bit here is that he says someone murdered your foster parents and the two of you covered it up because you wanted to keep on living at the farm. How do you explain that, Peter?"

"The ravings of a lunatic, I would say. Now, if you are not going to charge me with anything, I'm tired and hungry and would like to go home now please" said Corrigan.

Chamberlain's mobile pinged to indicate the arrival of a text. He retrieved the phone from his pocket. The text was from his boss, DCI Flemming.

My office please, now

"You are not going anywhere" he told Corrigan. "I will be back in a minute".

Chamberlain was slightly annoyed. He hadn't confronted Peter Corrigan about the stuff on the reverse of the mirror yet. He knew he would probably blame Neil for that as well but it would be more pressure on the man. It would have to wait. The implied tone of his boss's message meant he had to jump to it.

CHAPTER 31

"You have to let him go, Ralph" said DCI Flemming. She had been watching the interview on a video link.

"WHAT? No bloody way" exclaimed Chamberlain.

"Do you have any evidence directly linking Peter Corrigan to any of the murders?" she asked.

"Well…no, not exactly. Not yet" said a frustrated Chamberlain.

"Can you disprove any of the things he is telling you, about the Range Rover etc?"

"No"

"Then you can't hold him" she said, simply.

She was right and Chamberlain reluctantly knew she was right. He couldn't counter any of Peter Corrigan's fanciful answers to his questions. He either blamed his dead cousin….convenient…or had a rational, if false, answer for everything else.

"So what about Stan Hemmings? How do we

find him? I know he is a low down, drug dealing criminal but we still have to try to find him. And if it's not too late, save his life".

"I know, and I have a suggestion" said Flemming. "Have they started taking the Range Rover apart for forensics yet?"

"No, I don't think so. They are still working on his pick up at the moment" said Chamberlain.

"Then I will get authorisation to fit a tracker. Let him go and then we can see where he goes. How does that sound?" suggested Flemming.

"I love you, Detective Chief Inspector!"

"Steady there, DI Chamberlain. Let's not get carried away. What would Judith say if she knew?" quipped Flemming.

Judith. Chamberlain had put her to the back of his mind while he had been questioning Peter Corrigan. He should check on her.

"How long do you need to get the tracker authorised and then fitted?" he asked.

"Give it an hour to be safe" replied Flemming.

"Ok. Corrigan can stew for a while. I need to go and see Judith, make sure she's ok. If that's ok with you?"

"Go on, bugger off. Take her home. Give her

a hug from me. No more than that mind!" she said, mischievously.

Chamberlain would have loved nothing more than to take his love home and go to bed with her, even if it was just to cuddle and comfort her. Unfortunately that would have to wait. He went off to find Judith and take her home. She probably wouldn't want to go to his house after finding the letter.

He entered the room where she was still sleeping. It was a shame to wake her but she couldn't stay there. He went up to her and stroked her hair, then whispered...

"Judith, wake up, it's me"

She stirred, opened her eyes and smiled up at him. Then she yawned.

"How long have I been asleep" she enquired of him.

"I'm not sure exactly but probably a few hours. I need to take you home now. I have a bit of time before I am needed back here so Rebecca said I could go....well actually, she told me to bugger off and give you a hug" he said.

"Mmmm that sounds good" Judith said, sleepily.

Chamberlain was right. She didn't want to go to his place so he took her to her flat. Having settled her on the sofa he went and made her a hot chocolate drink. Coffee would not have been a good idea, just a stimulant. She needed to relax. He did have a coffee as he needed to stay awake.

She took a tentative sip of the hot, sweet liquid.

"Ahhh bisto?" she mimicked....or mocked, Chamberlain wasn't sure. She smiled. That was a good sign.

"I know you have probably decided against moving into the basement flat because of recent events" said Chamberlain "but what did you think of it, as a matter of interest?".

"It's lovely. It would be perfect. But as you say, I am not sure whether I could now, knowing that bloody Neil Corrigan has been in there. Snooping around and kidnapping poor Mrs Frobisher" she replied.

"Sure, I understand" said Chamberlain sadly.

"Don't let it to anyone else just yet though. Let me think about it. I am under pressure to find somewhere pretty quick so I won't write it off completely" added Judith. An ember of hope then.

This girl...this woman, was getting further and further under his skin. He had nearly lost her that night at Warwick Castle. He sat next to her for a while, in silence, just appreciating the warmth emanating from her...and the smell of her...a mix of natural odour and subtle remnants of a perfume. It felt good.

He would do his best not to fuck it up this time but for now he had a mission to get back to and she needed to rest.

They finished their drinks and he guided her to her bedroom and into bed. He wished he could join her, not just for sex but for the human contact and the reassurance that could bring. He snapped out of the thought and left her, snuggled up in the duvet. She was asleep before he even left the flat. Luckily it was a dreamless sleep as it could so have been full of nightmares.

Chamberlain left in his car and headed back to police HQ, wondering how the night was going to pan out. He had had enough of Corrigans. His determination rose and he sped up towards the station. What he could really do with was sitting in his armchair at home, generous tumbler of malt whisky, Oom Paul full of Capstan Navy Cut with Genesis wafting around his lounge…Afterglow, followed by Firth Of Fifth, would be a suitable choice. That would have to wait. Corrigan first, Genesis later…no, Corrigan first, then Judith and then Genesis.

CHAPTER 32

When Chamberlain got back to Warwick Police HQ he went straight to DCI Flemming's office and asked whether the tracker was fitted in the Range Rover. It was all ready to go so he went down to the interview room where Corrigan had been getting more and more impatient.

"So, Peter, sorry to keep you waiting" he said.

"About bloody time. I have been sitting here for ages. I need to go home" said Corrigan.

"Why the hurry Peter? You don't have any cows to tend anymore" stated Chamberlain.

"I'm tired and hungry" Corrigan said crossly. "I need to eat and I have things to sort out at the farm".

"Ok, you are free to go" Chamberlain said, simply. "Here are the keys to the Range Rover".

Corrigan looked at him suspiciously. Then he shrugged and took the keys, walked out of the open door and headed for the car park. He stoped half way to the exit door and turned back to look at Chamberlain.

"You really should take a holiday Inspector. You look terrible, you need a rest" and he smiled, turned again and went out of the door.

When Chamberlain got back to DCI Flemming's office he was furious.

"He really is an arrogant, self-assured, piece of shite. He knows we know but he also knows we have no proof. I just hope he doesn't give us the slip. How long is the battery life on that tracker?"

"I am told it should last about 6 hours. Given more time they could have fitted something more robust and long term but this is what we have to work with" said Flemming.

"Let's hope he leads us straight there, wherever 'there' is. How do we monitor the tracker?" asked Chamberlain.

"I've arranged for the feed to go into the big screen in the incident room. It should be ready for us now so let's go and have a look" replied Flemming.

They both left her office and went straight to the incident room where most of the team were at their desks. There was an air of uncertainty about the room. They tried to look busy when the senior officers entered the room but it didn't fool anyone.

"Ok, relax everyone. You are probably aware we have had to let Peter Corrigan go" There were murmurs around the room. Chamberlain raised his hands for quiet.

"Yes, I know, frustrating as hell. However, we have had a tracker fitted to his vehicle so he shouldn't be able to give us the slip. The feed should be up on the big screen. Norrish, can you sort that for us?" said Chamberlain.

DC Norrish nodded and got up to switch on the screen. Then he returned to his computer, tapped a few keys and as if by magic there was a map displayed for them, at the centre of which was their HQ building. A small red arrow was slowly moving away from them and heading through Warwick, going South West.

"It looks like he is heading out towards the Old Birmingham Road Sir" said DC Dixon.

They all just sat there for a while, watching the progress of the little red arrow. DCI Flemming had already put uniformed officers on alert so they were ready to pursue the target when ordered to do so. They didn't want to spook him but they also didn't want him to get away or to have time to get back to Hemmings, if he was still alive.

The little red arrow continued on its' journey, heading further out on the Old Birmingham Road. This made sense if Corrigan had diverted off this road earlier and was now heading back to the same place.

Then the arrow turned off the main road, at a place they all recognised.

"Shit! He's just gone back to the farmhouse" said Chamberlain. Had he misjudged this man? "Do we still have eyes on the farm?" he asked, to the room in general.

"Just regular drive-bys now sir. We don't have the resources to have permanent officers out there" answered Harris.

"Ok, stand down the troops, no point in re-arresting him now. Let me know the second he makes a move. I'm off for a smoke" said Chamberlain.

CHAPTER 33

At his farmhouse, Peter Corrigan was just sitting in an armchair, resting and gathering his thoughts. He was wondering why they had let him go so easily Had they really believed his answers to their questions? They actually had the story pretty much fully worked out with the help of his stupid little cousin, even though he was dead.

That Chamberlain was no idiot. Corrigan had been very careful that he wasn't followed when he had left the police building. Even so, he had gone straight to he farmhouse rather than returning to where he had left Stan Hemmings in the pine forest. He wondered if the man was still alive. It was several hours now since he had left him, without food or water. Corrigan didn't care about the man, per se. He did want to finish questioning him, just to make sure he had the right man.

He looked up at the wall where the mirror used to be. He should have been more careful and hidden it more effectively. He didn't need it anymore but it was somewhat incriminating he had to admit. It was also a record of his investigations. A bit of nostalgia.

He realised the whole thing was about to

collapse. He had to accept that. What he wouldn't accept was not being able to finish off properly. Put it all properly to bed. For Rob & Susan. It had all been done for them. All the planing, the research, the stalking, the killing. And now he was so close to the end.

He reflected on his life, most of which had been as a farmer. He enjoyed working with the cows and it had been a sad day, seeing his pride and joy herd being sold off. He wondered how they were being treated. He had treated them well. His little cousin Neil had not been so interested and had gone off to find a job 'in the real world' as he had called it. Well that had worked out well for him, hadn't it.

Thinking of Neil, Peter remembered his cousin's love of classical music, in particular the works of Gustav Mahler. He hadn't really shared the appreciation but he decided to put some on now. It was a bit gloomy and stormy for him but maybe it was appropriate for his mood.

His set the vinyl record going on the record deck and sat back in his armchair. All there was to drink was neat gin, no ice. He had poured himself a large slug and sipped at it as the music wafted around the room. The large mirror was gone, taken by the police as evidence, presumably. He should have hidden that better. Hindsight. Marvellous. Useless.

The gin started to take effect and he became drowsy, drifting into a semi-sleep. He dreamt of burial mounds and pre-historic skeletons. Had they been murder victims as well? Stories that would never be told. Would his story be told?

Peter Corrigan didn't view himself as a psychopath. He had to admit he was somewhat a serial killer. He had killed a series of low-life drug dealers so he supposed that counted, though he doubted many would mourn their loss. He had no sympathy for whatever might have driven them down the path they had followed.

He had never tried drugs himself. He liked a drink but not to excess. Running a farm meant early mornings and late nights. Having a hangover was not conducive to a successful and productive days work. A couple of times he had gone with Neil to the pub in town but he hadn't felt comfortable. People always wanted to know your business, where you were from, other personal details he wasn't prepared to share. He wasn't interested in them either. The one exception was when he had asked around as to where he could buy drugs as part of his search for dealers. All he got was funny looks.

His glass slipped from his hand, landing heavily on the floor but not breaking. The sound roused Corrigan from his dozing, the Mahler going through a quiet movement. That was enough depressing classical music. Rob and Susan had favoured more modern, up beat music. He flicked through their record collection and picked out one he knew they had loved. Joe Loss and his Orchestra from the Big Band Dance music of the 1940s. They would dance around the living room together to 'March Of

The Mods' or 'In The Mood'.

Peter Corrigan smiled at the memory. He and Neil would watch from the hallway, unbeknown to their foster parents who seemed to lose many of the hard years of farming and become young again to the music.

Anyway, that was all lost to the past now. Time to get back to Hemmings in the forest. He hope he was still alive and hadn't managed to escape. Corrigan was certain it was him and the other one, left dead in the workshop, that had ruined all of that life they had.

He locked up the farmhouse and got back into the Rage Rover. He was getting quite fond of the vehicle. Maybe he would get one, or keep this one. Not very practical around the farm but then he planned to disappear abroad after tonight. He drove away, thinking it might be the last time he saw the farm. Mixed memories and emotions taken away with him.

He drove down the farm track towards the main road and turned right, heading north, back towards the pine forest. He was fortunate that there were no patrol cars in either direction at that point. He managed to get all the way to the turn off without being seen. It was still dark, which helped. However, what he didn't know was that he was being tracked.

Having driven through the forest, navigating the increasingly rough tracks, he arrived back where he had left Stan Hemmings. He had driven off the track and into the forest a short way. When he got out and went over to where hemmings was tied to the tree, he was slumped over. Corrigan wasn't sure if he was asleep, unconscious or even dead. He gave the body a sharp kick. It groaned. Still alive then.

“Wakey wakey, I have some refreshments for you” he said.

“Fuck yuh” was the only response he got.

“Now, now. A bit of appreciation please. I have Ham and Egg or Chicken and Sweetcorn” he informed Hemmings. He got no response. “Ham and Egg then. That’s fine, I prefer the Chicken”.

He retrieved the shopping from the car and opened the sandwich carton. It was a tricky business feeding the restrained hemmings. He got a bit impatient waiting for the man to open his mouth and chew the food. He also gave him some water, though a lot of it spilled down the man’s front.

He gave up after a while and saw to his own hunger and thirst. When he had finished, he turned to Hemmings.

“Right. Now we are refreshed, we can carry on. No excuses now. I think time is running out for both of us” his tone had become more serious and threatening. Plenty more toes and fingernails to get through. He surveyed the tools available to him, thought for a moment and picked up the pliers.

CHAPTER 34

Chamberlain had spent longer than usual outside, smoking his pipe. In fact, he had treated himself to two bowls full. He tapped out the embers on the wall and put the pipe in his pocket, hoping it was cool enough not to burn a hole. Time to go back to the team and see what they were doing.

He made his way back into the building. It struck him how fond he was of Police HQ, Warwick. Silly really but his architecture appreciation side loved to know the history of buildings and their occupants. This one, for example, was a replacement for the original medieval Northgate buildings that were destroyed in the great fire of 1694. Stone built 'fire proof' high status town houses were occupied by various organisations from the 19th and 20th centuries, including the local militia, County Council and indeed, now, the area Police HQ.

Chamberlain wondered about the people who had occupied the buildings when they were residential houses. The great and the good of Warwick, he supposed.

Shaking off these thoughts, he headed for the incident room and his team. Just as he got into the room, his mobile rang. He answered quickly in case it was news. It was Richard Bewely, senior CSI.

"Hey, Richard. You must have something for me" said Chamberlain.

"Presumptuous, but, as ever, you are right old chap" replied Bewely "We have made quite few discoveries up at the farmhouse. Pretty much finished now so I can write my report but I thought I would give you a tinkle and feed you some headlines".

Pretentious public school prick thought Chamberlain. He knew the thought was hypocritical, having been to a public school himself but Richard Bewley had the affliction on another level.

"Ok, fire away" he said.

"Reed will be able to give you more, of course, once he gets his bits on the stuff" said Bewely, referring to the pathologist who did the post mortems,

"More bodies?" Asked Chamberlain with a feeling of dread.

"Bits of bodies, specifically fingers and teeth" answered Bewely "We found a crude incinerator behind one of the barns and on close inspection found dental and phalangeal remains, very charred. I know he's good but I wish Reed the best of luck identifying any of the owners of said remains".

"Sounds like it will keep him out of trouble for quite a while then" said Chamberlain.

"Ha ha ha" guffawed Bewely "Yes indeed, very good. We all found a large quantity of interesting paperwork and a small stash of cash, all of which has been boxed up and shipped back to base. Right, that's it for now" and he ended the call without ceremony.

Chamberlain stared at his phone. He hadn't thought his comment was that funny....not really funny at all but there was no figuring out some folks. He put the phone away in his jacket pocket. He had assumed there would be more information from Bewley following the thorough search of the farmhouse by the SOCOs. Maybe his full report would enlighten him further.

"Sir?" It was DC Dixon who interrupted his thoughts.

"Yup. What have you got?" he said.

"I have had quite a long conversation with Professor Reed. Apparently he is having quite a time of it down in autopsy. He says there is an awful lot of information to be gleaned but it is going to take some considerable time" Dixon said,

"I'm not surprised...and Bewley has a load more for him to sort out from the farmhouse" said Chamberlain.

"Apparently the forensic lab have been back to him with some results from remnants of hair. All of it shows signs of regular drug taking. Cannabis and cocaine. The drugs found with the bodies also go way beyond amounts for personal use" Dixon expanded.

"So we can probably assume these victims are drug dealers then" said Chamberlain "This is all backing up the information in the Neil Corrigan letter that Peter Corrigan is some kind of vigilante seeking revenge for the deaths of Robert and Susan Corrigan" said Chamberlain.

DC Norrish piped up. "Looks like it might be more than simple revenge killing sir. His search history on the laptop we recovered is very interesting. He was looking up methods of torture and butchering, by which I mean how to cut up a body neatly and efficiently. Very dark" Norrish had clearly been affected by the information he had discovered.

"He wanted to extract information from these dealers ...is that what we are saying?" said Chamberlain.

"Looks like it" answered Norrish.

Chamberlain decided he needed to speak to Professor Phillips, the university Forensic Psychologist. He went into his office and dialled the man's number.

"Inspector Chamberlain! Good to hear from

you as always" came the instant reply.

"Hi Professor, do you have a moment?" asked Chamberlain.

"Absolutely. How can I help?" he said. Chamberlain was always amazed at how willing this man was to help out, day or night, it seemed.

"Well, it looks like our suspect has been torturing his victims before killing them. Is this normal?"

"As you know, there is nothing normal, or standard, about psychopathic serial killers. It could be he is after information or he may just enjoy it. If the killings are some kind of mission...well, commonly, "invoking justifications" is a go-to strategy for serial killers. For example, so-called mission killers may insist that they're doing society a favour by helping to eliminate members of some "undesirable" target group" explained the Professor.

"That is becoming more and more likely I think. Ok, I won't keep you any longer...and thanks again for your help" Chamberlain ended the call.

"I am off to brief the DCI...back shortly" announced Chamberlain. He set off for her office. Her door was open and she was sat at her desk.

"Hey, how are you doing?" he asked.

"Well...you know..." she answered,

noncommittally.

Chamberlain didn't know but he wasn't going to press the matter. He knew she would talk to him about her health issues if she wanted to. Now was not the time.

"We are getting a fuller picture of events now" Chamberlain got straight to it. Flemming straightened her back and looked up, focus now on the case rather than her own problems. Chamberlain brought her up to date with all his team had gleaned from forensics, autopsy and the SOCOs at the farmhouse. He also relayed his conversation with Flemmings' friend Professor Phillips.

"So, the Corrigans are turning out to be quite a family" said Flemming "Just to recap…and correct me if I get anything wrong…we have a farming couple, getting on a bit, who foster and eventually adopt, two young troubled kids who both turn out to be psychopathic serial killers. Each one seems to have a different mission. Neil Corrigan was intent on getting to, and probably killing, you" Flemming paused and Chamberlain took a deep breath and sighed deeper. He couldn't argue with her so far.

"And then we have Peter Corrigan, his cousin or adoptive brother, whatever you want to call it…who seems to be on a vendetta to get revenge for the killing of Robert and Susan Corrigan by some crazed drug gang from Birmingham" said Flemming.

"Yes, pretty much. Two very different sets of victims. Neil's appeared to be random at first, until Mrs Frobisher, who was designed to get to me on a very personal basis. Peter, on the other hand, was specific in his targets and seems to have involved torture in order to extract information, possibly in order to find out exactly who killed his adoptive parents" said Chamberlain, for clarification.

"To use the vernacular....what a cluster fuck!" said Flemming, using a phrase that would not appear in any official reports but did actually describe the situation pretty well, thought Chamberlain.

"Well, quite" he replied "There is still a mountain of evidence to go through, including trying to identify all the victims in the freezer but all that is going to take weeks. We could do with some help going through all the documentation from the farm house. It's still a mystery to me how the two boys kept the farm going all those years without really being noticed".

"I'll request some more help from uniform" said Flemming.

Chamberlain thanked her and left her office, wondering how she was really doing. He couldn't imagine what it must be like going through the diagnosis of cancer and the realisation that you might not make it through the treatment. He felt for his pipe in his pocket and was about to head out for a smoke but changed his mind. Someone once said it was bad for you and although he didn't inhale the smoke, he was aware that it could cause mouth or throat cancer.

He got back to the team and they settled in for another session of studying all the evidence. There was more from forensics and from autopsy.

Going through all the stuff from the farmhouse, the CSIs had discovered some very interesting paperwork, going back many years. For a start, they had found signed adoption papers for both Neil and Peter Corrigan. That made sense but what didn't fit was the date of the signatures. If Robert and Susan Corrigan had been killed approximately twenty years ago, then they could not have signed the adoption papers thirteen years ago. The boys , or one of them, must have forged their signatures.

Another interesting and useful piece of evidence was a little black book, one of those called Moleskin, with the elastic page marker. It was full of passwords and bank on line access details for Robert and Susan. It was becoming more and more apparent how the two boys had managed to maintain the illusion that Robert and Susan were still alive.

From autopsy and Professor Daniel Reed, came news that although nothing was fully confirmed, they were starting to match up body parts and link them with potential missing person reports from all over the West Midlands, in particular, Birmingham. There would however, be many more weeks of DNA testing and matching before they had the full picture.

CHAPTER 35

Judith had arrived for her next therapy session with Dr. Samantha Howard. They had booked it for very soon after the last one as both hadn't wanted to lose momentum with the therapy and the progress they had made so far. Judith was slightly apprehensive as Samantha had warned her that this next session might be quite hard going. She wondered what that would entail. They settled in their usual positions on the comfortable furniture in the therapy room. It was more like a lounge really and Judith immediately felt at ease.

"So, Judith. Let's get straight to it" she wasn't hanging around.

"Oookay" Judith replied, hesitantly.

"I want you to talk me through the events of that night, in detail, and tell me what you were thinking all the way through...right up to the point where you were rescued" said Sam.

"Fooph! Ok. Where shall I start?" asked Judith.

"Why not start at the restaurant where you were with Ralph...and don't leave anything out" instructed Sam "And I want to hear about what you were feeling emotionally as well, not just a list of what happened" she added.

Judith sat back and thought for a few moments. Sam had been right. This was not going to be easy. She took a deep breath.

"Ok...we met at the restaurant. I was nervous about how the evening might go. I didn't really know what I wanted to happen. I knew I was attracted to Ralph but was it just physical? Did he like me? Was that just physical?" she started off.

She spent the next forty minutes or so going over the meal, what they had eaten, what they had talked about. She had been feeling happy and almost schoolgirlish in her attraction to Ralph. He was good company and a good conversationalist. Relaxed. That was it, she felt relaxed in his company. Then she got the bit when she got up and went to the ladies room. She paused, trying to remember exactly what had happened and what she had been feeling.

"I think at the time, I was worrying about what was going to happen next...between Ralph and me, I mean. Would he ask me back to his? Would he want to sleep with me? Did I want to sleep with him? Was it too soon? That kind of thing. Then I saw this man at the back, by the staff entrance. He seemed to be having trouble, I thought he was ill so I went up to him' she paused again.

"No rush, take your time" said Sam.

She described, as best she could, how she had approached the man, asking if he had been ok. The next bit was a blur. The man had suddenly stood up and put something over her mouth and nose. The next she knew was when she started to come round, finding herself suspended, with her arms above her head, on some battlements, overlooking the river. She had been groggy and had no clue what was going on. The scene that unfolded before her, through groggy mists, was that of a man standing by the battlements talking to Ralph who seemed to be restrained up against the main wall of the castle.

"I was terrified and at the same time confused" she explained to Sam "I was slipping in and out of a foggy sort of consciousness...." She seemed to be reliving the experience in her head and fell silent for a few moments. Sam said nothing, not wanting to interrupt the flow of thoughts and feelings.

"When I was strung up there, I was scared, obviously, but also had great feelings of sadness. If I was going to die then what might I be missing out on with Ralph. I realised I was falling for this guy, big time"

"I was worried it might just be a fragile victim/ hero obsession but I think you have dispelled that theory for me...and for yourself" Sam smiled.

"Then, when I saw him go over the

battlements....I thought I would lose him. I panicked and struggled against my bindings but I couldn't escape. I couldn't help him" Judith felt tears running down her cheeks and wiped them away, briskly.

"It's ok for you to cry, Judith. In fact it is good for you. I would be worried if the experience and all the emotions didn't make you shed a few tears" said Sam.

"It became clear to me that Ralph had come to rescue me....it was my fault for being so careless at the restaurant" said Judith.

"No, Judith. None of it was your fault, not Ralph's. The blame falls firmly with this Neil Corrigan character, I can assure you" replied Sam, firmly.

"Thank you" said Judith, quietly. "I also worry that the reason we have started to become so close is because of the shared events of that night. I mean, would that have happened without me being kidnapped and my 'hero' coming to the rescue? Isn't there some kind of syndrome associated with such things?" queried Judith.

"Well, there is, yes. To be honest, there are syndromes for everything in life and I don't always think it is helpful to put labels on things. It may well have brought you two closer but without the original attraction and spark, it wouldn't last. I believe you are both above any of that" assured Sam.

Judith suddenly let out a huge sigh and leant

back in her seat. She felt lighter, exhausted and somehow clearer in her head. She managed a smile.

"You were right. Todays session was hard work!"

"By the look of you, it was well worth it...and timely" said Sam.

"I also think I might be able to write my article now. I had some kind of mental blockage before but getting it all off my chest has freed me up, somehow" said Judith.

"That's great. Getting the story down on paper, as it were, will further help with your recovery, I'm sure" added Sam

"So, do we need to keep on with these sessions?" asked Judith.

"Up to you, really. Why don't we leave it a while. We can book one for a couple of months as back up, just in case things don't go as smoothly as we hope" said Sam.

Judith knew she really meant if she had a relapse. It made sense, however you put it so they agreed on a date on the proviso that if Judith felt she didn't need the extra session, they could cancel it. Judith knew she would miss talking to this woman.

"Fancy going out for a drink sometime? Maybe I could get Rebecca Flemming along as well. She is

Ralph's DCI but I have known her for years" suggested Judith.

"Why not?" replied Sam. She wasn't usually in the habit of fraternising with clients but she felt they had made great progress and was pretty sure they weren't going to need the back up session. In fact, meeting up in a social situation could easily replace the formal setting they normally met in, just for a catch up, anyway.

CHAPTER 36

Corrigan tightened the rope around Stan Hemmings's neck. He needed to finish this quickly. The dark night sky was turning pale and the birds were waking up with their morning songs. He had fed his prisoner half of the sandwich and given him some water so he had revived a little. Enough to answer some final questions.

For good measure he set about his victim again, causing him considerable pain. The toe crushing seemed to cause the most discomfort in the man. Corrigan found it interesting how people differed in their response to his type of questioning. He had done quite a lot of research over the years...and quite a lot of experimenting. He felt he was pretty good at it now.

The skill, in his opinion, was to cause a lot of pain but not so much as to render the subject unconscious...or dead, at least not initially. He now had a whole host of methods in his arsenal. Fingernails were a good one. Genitals another. Sometimes just the threat of hurting these was enough to illicit the right response.

He subjected a couple more toes to the pliers. Then Hemmings vomited, the recent sandwich and other stomach contents ending up in his lap. Corrigan was getting more and more frustrated.

"For fuck's sake, I know it was you who killed my foster parents. You and that waste of space friend of yours with the dreadlocks. You may as well admit it" Corrigan said.

By now, Stan Hemmings was weak and fading fast. His brain was somewhat befuddled and his vision was blurring. Sub-consciously he had given up. He just wanted an end to the torture, whatever that end might be.

"Yea mi kill dem deh fuckas, suh fuck yuh" Stan said, almost in a whisper.

"What's that now?"

"Mi kill dem.... dem double cross wi" said Hemmings.

"They refused to let you grow your disgusting drugs in their barn?" suggested Corrigan.

"Yuh. Couldn't ave dem blabbing bout di scheme eff dem weren't pan board" confirmed Hemmings.

"And there it is. That wasn't so hard was it?" Corrigan sat back from the position he had been in, squatting on his haunches. After all these years he finally had confirmation, from the horses mouth, as to who had committed the foul murder all those years ago. He felt vindicated.

He was about to deliver the coup de grace when he noticed how light it was getting. People might be coming out to give their dogs a morning walk. He made a decision. He gathered up the tools and battery lantern and put them in the back of the Range Rover. Then he undid the rope around the tree and bundled Hemmings onto the back seats again, to the sounds of much groaning and probably cursing, though he couldn't understand most of it.

"Be quiet or it's more chloroform for you" he ordered his prisoner. He got a grunt in response.

"Good boy" said Corrigan.

He got in the driver seat and started the engine. It really was getting light now. He drove off and out along the forestry tracks and onto the main road. He had to drive north a short way before he came to a track on the right which led across his land towards the copse. He was vaguely aware of the distant noise of a helicopter way up in the sky. He paid no attention to it, concentrating on the rugged track he had turned into, off the main road.

Shortly, the track faded out and he was crossing fields and going through gaps in hedges. This was all still land owned by his farm. There seemed to be lots of options and settings for particular terrains for the Range Rover but Corrigan didn't have time to work them out. He just needed to get to the copse.

Once there, he would kill Hemmings, do

the usual dismembering, which, although no longer strictly necessary, had become part of his MO. Then he would bury the evidence and head off into the sunset, as it were. This was all assuming he had enough time. The hairs on the back of his neck were up and he felt as if he was being followed, and that they were getting closer and closer.

He pressed on across the farmland. He would miss the fields and woods around the place. He had spent over two decades on the farm and considered it his home. It was, of course, all Neil's fault that everything was coming crashing down. He, Peter, had been getting along just fine with his endeavours. It was very unlikely that he would have been caught if Neil hadn't become obsessed with this Chamberlain character and drawn attention to other things happening at the farm. Stupid little fucktard.

CHAPTER 37

As Corrigan was driving across his fields towards the copse, DI Chamberlain and DS Harris were driving through the pine forest, searching for the last known location of the Range Rover. The tracks were getting rougher as they got further into the forest and Chamberlain's car was not best suited to rough tracks. He had to slow right down to avoid bottoming out and potentially ripping off the exhaust pipe or damaging the suspension.

Unfortunately the tracker battery had run out some half an hour previously so they had no idea whether Corrigan was still where it last said he was. He wasn't.

"Bugger. He's gone" said Chamberlain "Let's have a look around anyway".

Harris had brought a tablet with him which had shown the live link from the tracker when it was live. It had a bigger screen that his movie phone so was easier to follow. He was more tech savvy than his boss so he was in charge of that while Chamberlain drove.

They both got out of the car and started to look around the area. There were definitely tyre tracks leading off the rough forestry road. They followed them into the trees, on foot. There was no way Chamberlain was going to go off track in his car. They didn't have to walk far.

"Tyre tracks stop here, sir" said Harris.

There was an area where the dead pie needles on the forest floor had clearly been disturbed. It looked like something heavy had been dragged across the forest floor to the base of a large pine tree.

"There's a bit of rope on the ground behind this tree with what looks like blood on it" said Chamberlain.

"Do you think Hemmings is dead sir?" asked Harris.

"Probably" came the reply.

"Empty sandwich carton over here sir" said Harris. They recognised it as one of the two that Corrigan had had in his shopping bag. "Ham and egg".

"Call the SOCOs in will you, Tom. We need to try and figure out where he would have gone. If Hemmings is dead he will need to get rid of the body somewhere. Let's have a look at the Google maps thing and see if there is anywhere else on the farm that he might go to as he seems to like to keep his activities in house, so to speak" said Chamberlain.

They went and sat in the car and Chamberlain

waited for Harris to get the map up on screen. He had cleverly overlain the farm boundaries from the Land Registry so they could see the area they were dealing with.

"He probably won't want to go far" said Chamberlain.

"Ok, well here we are in the pine forest" said Harris, pointing at the map.

"Can you zoom out a bit so we can see the whole area?" asked Chamberlain.

Harris used his forefinger and thumb to squeeze the map so they got the full view. They could see the farmhouse and slightly to the south east was the small wood where the burial mounds were located and the whole saga had started with the two poachers.

"Ok, somewhere isolated and not obvious from the main road" said Chamberlain. They both stared at the screen for a while. Then Harris pointed at something.

"See this, out in the middle of the fields? Some kind of small bit of woodland. Away from everything else" he said.

"A copse" said Chamberlain. He had a thing about copses. His elder brother had told him that a copse near where they grew up, and passed everyday on the way to school, was full of wolves and he should never go there. At the time it terrified him. He learned later that it was where his brother went to meet his mates and smoke fags and drink beer. He just didn't want his little brother disturbing him. There was still a lingering notion of wolves whenever Chamberlain saw a copse, however irrational.

"That's where I would choose, Sir" said Harris.

"I agree. I think we are going to need a better suited vehicle. Corrigan has a Range Rover, we are in a saloon car. Do we have any 4x4s still in the local pool?" said Chamberlain.

"I think the old Defender is still around. Shall I find out? said Harris.

"Yes. If it is available, get someone to drive it out here and meet us at the forest entrance" ordered Chamberlain.

A Land Rover Defender would be just the job for getting across farmland and through woodland. The world renowned utility vehicle, originally designed in 1947, inspired by a Jeep axle and chassis, was created by engineer and Rover Company Chairman Maurice Wilks, while he was with his brother Spencer on their farm in Wales.

Their use was so widespread due to their versatility, ruggedness and ease of maintenance. Favoured by explorers, armies, police forces, rescue services, farmers and a whole community of pure enthusiasts. Many changes and improvements had happened over the decades of course. The Defender had been a reliable tool for all sorts of aspects of policing including crowd and riot control.

Chamberlain needed this one to follow a psychopathic serial killer across his own farmland. Harris made the call.

“We are in luck sir. The Defender is still operational and is available. A uniform will drive it up here now. They reckoned about 20-25 minutes” Harris told his boss.

“Brilliant. I just hope we are not too late and have picked the right spot” said Chamberlain in response. “Put in a request to get the helo to fly over the area and see if there is any sign”

While Harris put in the request, Chamberlain drove back out through the forest and parked up at the entrance and waited. It was actually only 15 minutes later when the Defender arrived. The driver must have put his foot down. Not much traffic either, at that time of night.

They swapped vehicles, Chamberlain driving. The distinctive roar of the Land Rover increasing as he sped off up the Old Birmingham Road. He kept the blues and twos off for the time being as he didn’t want to give Peter Corrigan too much warning that they were after him. Chamberlain wasn’t one hundred percent they were going to the right place in any case.

The vehicles’ police radio burst into life.

"Dark coloured vehicle spotted at target location. Please confirm orders" said the voice from the helicopter.

"Tell them to hold back but keep eyes on" instructed Chamberlain. Harris relayed the order to their airborne colleagues.

"Right, let's get the bugger!" shouted Chamberlain as he accelerated up the road towards where they now knew Corrigan to be located. The Land Rover was a great vehicle but handling at speed was not its' greatest asset. In the passenger seat, DS Tom Harris was gripping the arm rest with white knuckles. If Chamberlain had been able to look at his face he would have seen a vision of terror.

It's a rare thing for a driver, however good they may be, to appreciate how their passenger might be feeling, particularly when speed is the essence. Chamberlain was so focussed on catching up with Peter Corrigan that he gave no thought to how DS Tom Harris might, or might not, be coping with the journey. This was ironic really, as Chamberlain himself hated being driven. He was the worlds' worst passenger.

Luckily there wasn't a lot of traffic on the Old Birmingham road as they sped along. Looking down at the speedo, Chamberlain noticed…along with the speed of 95 miles per hour…that there was very little fuel left in the vehicle.

"For fuck's sake" he cursed.

"What's that now, sir?" quivered Harris.

"Fuel...almost out of fuel" shouted Chamberlain.

Harris was about to reply that as the Land Rover wasn't used much, those in charge of the pool probably hadn't bothered to keep her fuelled up. They certainly hadn't had time to check before delivering the vehicle to them. Harris decided not to state the bleeding obvious. It wouldn't help his boss's demeanour... or driving, for that matter.

"There's usually more than you think in the tank sir" said Harris, hopefully. Privately and selfishly he rather hoped they would run out. At least they might survive!

They neared what they thought would be the access track to lead them across the farmland to where Corrigan had been spotted. To Harris's relief, Chamberlain slowed the vehicle to a more acceptable speed as he turned off the main road. However, as they hit the farm track, Chamberlain gunned the engine once more and they bounced along the rough surface.

Harris wasn't a religious man but he did send out a silent prayer just in case there was a celestial or spiritual being that could keep them on track... literally. He looked across again at his boss. There was a look on his face that Harris didn't recognise. Determined but also slightly murderous, if he wasn't mistaken. Maybe it was just concentration on the tricky task at hand, that of proceeding at speed across rough terrain after a homicidal maniac. If you put it like that then any facial expression was acceptable. Harris looked forwards again and concentrated on keeping his sandwich down in his stomach where it belonged.

CHAPTER 38

It was fully daylight now but Corrigan wasn't worried about that. These fields were not frequented by dog walkers and the copse was not really big enough to be of interest to anyone. Perfect for Corrigan though. He arrived at the edge of the trees and pulled under the canopy and stopped the vehicle.

"Here we are then. Hopefully we won't be disturbed out here" he said to himself more than anything. He got out and went to the back of the vehicle and retrieved the tool bag. He would only need one of them really but he intended to leave the bag in the woods, buried with Stan Hemmings.

"Out you come then" he said to his captive. He had to drag the man from the back seats, unceremoniously dumping him on the ground. He stretched his back before grabbing the mans collar and heaving him further into the shelter of the copse. It was a remnant of the huge forest that used to cover the area and some of the trees were very old.

He quickly reached the middle of the copse and propped Hemmings up against an old Beech tree. He removed the tape from Hemmings's mouth.

"Any famous last words?" he enquired.

"Fuck yuh, yuh cyaa just kill mi!" entreated Hemmings.

"Yeah, sure I can. Like you killed my foster parents, Rob and Susan" said Corrigan. It seemed reasonable to him. He had been circling his victim slowly, one of the tools in his hand. He heard the noise in the sky again. This time he looked up with interest. Still some distance away he spotted a helicopter. There were blue flashing lights on it. Police.

"Damn!" Corrigan wasn't ready. He needed time for the kill and then more time to bury the evidence. He would have to get a move on.

"I would say I'm sorry" he said before striking Hemmings on the back of the head "but I am not sorry. Not one little bit". Hemmings had slumped forward and rolled on to his back. Corrigan didn't know if he was dead yet but the noise of the helicopter was getting nearer and louder.

Stan Hemings hadn't had to summon his survival instincts for some while. He usually had BJ for that. For the time being it seemed sensible to 'play dead' if he had any chance of avoiding actually being dead. His attacker was distracted by the noise of an approaching helicopter. He was praying it was the police, not something he was used to wanting but this was different.

The blow to the head he had just received hurt

like hell and he had thought he was going to pass out. However, he hadn't. Maybe the man hadn't meant to kill him or had just misjudged the force of the blow. Anyway, it took all of Stan's self control to not move a muscle and play dead.

The helicopter was almost overhead now. Another sound joined that of the rotors. Stan recognised the labouring strains of a Land Rover making its' way across the fields towards them. He heard the man curse.

"Fuck....you bastards. How did you find me so quickly" said Corrigan. He turned and looked down at Hemmings. He didn't have time to make sure the man was dead. He had to make a run for it. He jumped into the Range Rover and gunned the engine. He decided to go through the woods in the opposite direction to the approaching vehicle. He realised his only chance was to get away from the copse and make it to the larger woods across the fields. He could lose them in there, he was sure.

As he exited the copse, a great shadow hovered over him. A very noisy shadow, being that of the police helicopter. He floored the accelerator and vehicle lurched forward, bouncing over the rutted ground. He was guessing the helicopter would be unable to stop him, just shadow him while the ground forces caught up, so he had to keep going. He didn't know how far behind him they were, he couldn't see or hear them yet.

He just focused on his target the other side

of the field, some 300 yards away. If he could get there.....As he bounced across the field he could still hear the thud..thud of the helicopter above him. He accelerated as much as he dared on the rough terrain. A great vehicle but ploughed fields gave anything a run for its' money.

Corrigan just hoped he had hit Stan Hemmings hard enough to kill him. He didn't like it. It was an untidy end to his pursuit of justice for Rob and Susan. He realised he always knew and accepted that he would get caught eventually but now it came to it, his self-preservation instincts had kicked in. He wasn't going to make it easy for them.

If he could get to the woods....After that he wasn't sure but one thing at a time. He knew his way around better than anybody. He was sure he could outrun and outsmart his pursuers. Damn that bloody Chamberlain! Why couldn't he just let him get on with his mission. He was doing society a favour, right? Yes, there was a revenge element to what he was and had been doing but it was all for Robert and Susan.

CHAPTER 39

A message came through on the police radio from the helicopter to Chamberlain and Harris in the Land Rover.

"Subject vehicle has exited the copse and heading across the fields" said the comms officer in the helicopter.

"Tell him to keep eyes on, and update us with his movements" Chamberlain told Harris, who relayed the message.

They were bouncing along at some speed but very little comfort. The police Land Rover was efficient but not smooth. Chamberlain had his advanced police driving qualification but there had been little instruction about driving across rough, rutted farmland. If he had looked across at Harris he would have seen a very concerned expression.

"Have you still got that Google Earth image on your iPad?" asked Chamberlain.

"Yes Sir" came the reply.

Chamberlain slowed to a halt to give them both

a chance to look at the screen without it jumping up and down. They could clearly see the Copse situated in the middle of a field. They could also see a much larger bit of woodland on the far side of the field. If they let Corrigan get in there, it would be nigh impossible to catch up with him.

"We have to stop him before he reaches those woods. Hold on to your hat, Tom" Chamberlain drove off again, at speed. He was going to drive around the copse rather than go through it. Further distance-wise but quicker on open, albeit rough, terrain.

The Land Rover was bouncing its' way across the rutted field and Tom's head kept hitting the roof. Chamberlain didn't have time for sensibilities. Corrigan was not going to get away. He gritted his teeth and accelerated some more. If he had had a hat, Harris would certainly have had a firm grip on it. There was equipment in the back of the Land Rover that had been stowed properly but was now flying all over the place.

As luck would have it, Corrigan had aimed the Range Rover towards the left as he exited the copse. He knew of a way through the woods in that direction. Chamberlain had chosen to circle the copse to the left. This meant that he had already closed the angle and therefore the distance between them. As he cleared the edge of the copse he caught sight of the fleeing vehicle about 150 yards ahead of them.

"There he is, sir" shouted Harris,

enthusiastically, and somewhat unnecessarily.

They could now see the Range Rover speeding across the field, still being shadowed by the helicopter above. There wasn't much they could do in terms of helping the pursuit, other than keep track of the vehicle on the ground. It would be more difficult once he hit the trees.

"Do they have heat seeking cameras on that chopper?" asked Chamberlain.

"I'm not sure, shall I ask them?" replied Harris.

"Don't bother, he won't get that far" said a determined Chamberlain.

One problem with the Range Rover was that it had low profile road tyres fitted, mainly because Stan thought they looked cool. They did. However, it meant that, despite the fancy 4x4 options on the Vogue, it wasn't great in driving at speed across open, rutted fields. If Peter Corrigan had been familiar with the controls and options he might have had time to select a more appropriate drive. He wasn't, and he didn't. He had the advantage of power and comfort but only really in a proper road environment. He was struggling to keep the vehicle going in the direction he wanted. He was cursing.Looking in his rear view mirror he saw that he was now being followed on the ground as well as in the air.

"Fuck, fuck, fuck" he continued cursing. If he could only get to the tree line he might stand a chance.

Looking back again, he saw that his pursuer had closed on him. He wasn't going to make it. He made a decision. He would have to try to take the pursuer out. He swung the wheel over to the left and aimed the Range Rover directly at his enemy's vehicle.

"Jesus, he is driving straight at us" exclaimed Harris. He looked across at his boss whose expression was determined. His hands gripped the steering wheel tighter and he didn't waiver in his direction. They were now in a very dangerous game of chicken.

"Sir…" started Harris, then decided better of it.

"Jump out Harris" shouted Chamberlain.

"What? No way" replied Harris.

"No point in risking both of us going down. Jump….NOW"

Harris hesitated, then unclipped his seatbelt, grabbed the door handle, pulled it and the door came open. He hesitated again, then felt a shove from behind. He flew out of the moving vehicle and landed painfully on his left shoulder and heard a crack. He very nearly passed out with the pain but managed to sit up as the Land Rover continued its' way towards the oncoming Range Rover. He watched in horror.

The police Land Rover was fitted with off road tyres so therefore had much better grip on the current terrain. Chamberlain fixed his eyes on the oncoming vehicle.

"Come on then, you wacko" he said, not sure if he meant Corrigan or himself. He wasn't sure if he had the balls not to swerve but he was certainly going to do his best.

As it turned out, they both swerved at the last second. However, Chamberlain swerved to his left and Corrigan swerved to his right. This meant they were still going to collide, though maybe in slightly less dramatic fashion than a full head on smash.

In fact, what happened was quite spectacular in that when they collided, the robust Land Rover front offside wheel arch hit the Range Rover and smashed the suspension, creating immediate instability for its' driver. Chamberlain caught a glimpse of Corrigan desperately struggling to control the Range Rover, without success. Both vehicles tipped over. The Range Rover so much so that it rolled over twice before coming to a stop on its' roof.

The Land Rover went over on to one side and stopped abruptly as the front nearside wing dug into the ground.

Chamberlain had been wearing his seatbelt. Corrigan had not.

Chamberlain was dazed and bruised but conscious. He was half suspended by his belt and was struggling to free himself. Then, suddenly, Harris appeared above him, clutching his left arm. He managed to get the driver door open and help Chamberlain out on to the ground.

"Are you ok sir? That was one hell of a crash!" said Harris.

"Bit dazed Tom…think I bumped my head" Chamberlain said rather woozily.

He staggered over to the up-turned Range Rover which had steam coming out from the engine compartment. The windscreen and both side windows were smashed in. He bent down and looked inside. Corrigan was on his back, on the roof of the cab, blood coming from somewhere. Lots of blood. His eyes were closed.

"He looks a lot worse than either of us" said Chamberlain. He was about to turn away when there was a groan from inside the vehicle. He turned back and looked at Corrigan. His eyes were now open.

"Well played, Inspector" croaked Corrigan. Then his eyes glazed over and he was gone. There was nothing they could do for him.

Chamberlain walked a short distance and then sat down on the ground. He felt in his trouser pocket for his pipe. Then he frowned and pulled out two separate pieces. During the crash his beloved pipe had snapped in two.

"Shit" he said, apparently more annoyed about this loss than the near fatal crash he had just been through.

"I can see the back up vehicles arriving at the copse now sir" said Harris.

"Stan Hemmings must still be in there somewhere as there is no one else in the Range Rover" said Chamberlain. "He is probably dead as well".

Harris and Chamberlain just sat together in the middle of the field, both rather dazed after the experience. Then they saw a lone figure stumble out of the copse, walk a few paces, then collapse on the ground. It was Stan Hemmings.

The helicopter that had been circling above and had not only seen but had filmed the action below them, started to descend some 100 yards away from them. It landed and someone leapt out and rushed towards them. It was DCI Rebecca Flemming.

"Ralph!" she shouted "Are you ok? What the fuck were you thinking?" Whilst relieved she was clearly annoyed at his recklessness.

"I'm ok, just a bit bruised. Corrigan is dead" he stated, simply.

"You're lucky you aren't dead! And as for pushing Harris out of a moving vehicle....well, maybe you saved his life" she conceded.

"Split second decision. Ma'm" he replied. "I did try to take evasive action, as you will have seen, as did Corrigan. Just turned out we swerved in the same direction"

“Yes, yes, I saw it all from above” said Flemming.

Chamberlain had a thumping headache and needed to sit down, which he did rather unceremoniously on the ground. He put one hand to his head and rubbed his temple. What he would give for a functional pipe and a good smoke.

“We need to get you two to hospital for a check over” said Flemming.

Rather than trying to be the nonchalant hero, Chamberlain agreed. His sergeant definitely needed his arm and shoulder looking at. While they waited for someone to pick them up he rang Judith who was relieved to hear he was ok and that Corrigan would no longer be a threat to anyone.

“Playing the bloody hero again, I suppose” she said angrily. However relieved she was, she would not let him off his recklessness. She realised this man meant a lot to her now and she wanted him back safe and sound.

“Just doing my job....” Then he passed out and crumpled to one side, dropping his phone and leaving Judith wondering what had happened.

Epilogue

Chamberlain was taking a smoking break in the car park at Police HQ, Warwick, when DCI Flemming arrived. She parked, got out of her car and walked over to him.

"Morning Sherlock" she said, grinning. He hadn't had time to buy a new 'everyday' pipe so he had his Oom Paul out in public, the distinctive bowl and curved stem giving him a certain air. All he needed was a deerstalker hat to finish off the picture.

"Shut ya face...Ma'm" he said, seriously. She knew it would wind him up, knowing his dislike of fictional detectives, Conan Doyle or not. There were a number of fictional sleuths and Detectives who smoked pipes, Sherlock Holmes and Maigret among them. However, Chamberlain was not trying to emulate any of them. He just liked smoking a pipe.

"When you have finished sleuthing....I mean, smoking, can you pop into my office for a word please?" She sounded a little more serious now.

No peace for the wicked he thought. He took his time and enjoyed the full bowl's worth of his Capstan Navy Cut pipe tobacco. It had been a hectic and harrowing few weeks. So much had happened since he got back from his holiday in Barcelona. It seemed like a lifetime ago. In that short time, he and his team had had to deal with 2 psychopathic serial killers, both bearing the name of Corrigan. In amongst that, he seemed to have gained a girlfriend. Judith Webster, one of a breed that Chamberlain was known to dislike, that of journalists.

He puffed the final puff, then tapped out the ash against the side of the building and put the pipe in his pocket. Hopefully it wouldn't burn a hole. He then made his way up to his boss's office. She was waiting patiently for him.

"I wanted to wait until after this Corrigan business was wrapped up to tell you. It looks like we are moving HQ out to Leek Wootton" said DCI Flemming.

"I suppose this place is a bit tired...and we could do with more space" said Chamberlain. "Not so central, but then we haven't had a front desk as such for quite a while". Chamberlain did privately wonder whether the fact that there was a golf course right next to the new HQ had anything to do with the decision by the top brass to move out there.

Over the last few years many smaller and some larger police stations had either been closed down or at least had the public access front desk removed. More budget cuts and streamlining. Chamberlain felt it only served to remove the police further away from the public. He just about remembered the days when each village had its' own bobby.

"I wonder what will happen to this place when we have gone" mused Chamberlain.

"Rumour has it that it will be redeveloped and will revert to residential use. Back to being town houses maybe? They would probably sell for a fortune nowadays" replied Flemming.

"Funny, I was just thinking about who would have lived here when they were originally built, after the fire" said Chamberlain. DCI Flemming wasn't that interested if she was honest. He had a sudden thought...he wouldn't be able to use the cafe around the corner as his satellite office. He would miss that option...and their coffee and buns. He had a fleeting casual thought as to why it seemed that cafes were always 'just around the corner'. He wondered what the new place could offer in terms of somewhere to escape.

"The Defender is fine, by the way. Just new bolt on front wings and replacement lights, that's all" said Flemming.

"Good news. You never know when you might need to call on such a vehicle. I hope they don't retire it any time soon" replied Chamberlain.

"Well, it certainly came off a lot better than the modern Range Rover...as did its' occupant" added Flemming.

"You know, we almost ran out of fuel!" said Chamberlain "Probably a good thing we had an almost empty fuel tank. Could have been nasty in a crash like that"

"Lucky it was a diesel vehicle as well" added Flemming.

"I wonder what will happen to the farm. Sold off I expect" said Chamberlain.

"It's a sad reflection on the world that nobody seemed to notice the disappearance of Rob & Susan Corrigan, not even officialdom. I suppose it is increasingly a faceless society. You can't see a bank manager anymore, can you" reflected Flemming.

"You know the dig in the woods is going to be on the telly?" said
Chamberlain.

"So I gather. They have made some interesting finds as I understand it. It's made some additions to local history for the boffins and local history enthusiasts" said Flemming.

"Fame and notoriety at the same time!" Chamberlain added.

His passing interest in archaeology drew him to wonder if he would be able to go and see the dig without it being tainted with the memory of how his old housekeeper, Mrs Frobisher, had met her horrific end at the hands of Neil Corrigan. Maybe one day, it was too soon at the moment.

It was indeed a rare find for the area which would've been part of the former Forest Of Arden. This was thought to have been sparsely populated and poor in agriculture, covering a large amount of Warwickshire up to and including Roman times. Even for Willian Shakespeare, in the 16th/17th century, it had been an important part of his youth and the scene for some of his plays.

——-

Stan Hemmings was still just about alive when the paramedics got to him on the edge of the copse where he had collapsed. He was in one hell of a state. Corrigan had crushed six of his toes and ripped out three finger nails. Then there were the head wounds. The first time Corrigan had hit him, back at the workshop, it had just knocked him out and left a nasty bruise and a bump.

The second time, which had been meant as the kill blow, had cracked his skull but not enough to kill him. There was significant swelling of the brain. He was unconscious when they got to him and they were amazed he had managed to stumble as far as he had. He was taken straight to the nearest head trauma unit in Birmingham. It was touch and go as to whether he would pull through and there were probably going to be long term effects on memory and mobility. They wouldn't know for some time. He was certainly in no condition to be interviewed by the police.

The local police up in the Nechells suburb of Birmingham eventually found the buried container behind Stan Hemmings's workshop. They considered it a great hall. There was the weaponry and about £5m street value in cannabis and cocaine. A considerable amount of weapons and drugs now off the streets making the area just a little bit safer. They knew if was the tip of the iceberg, of course but every little bit helped. Even if one person was stopped from being shot and one overdose avoided, that was a result.

Stan was going to be spending many years behind bars, once he was out of hospital, so the workshop and all the cars were seized by the state.

They would be sold off as the proceeds of organised crime. He was charged with various drug and firearms offences but even when offered a deal, he refused to give away any information about the larger OCG involved higher up the chain.

Hemmings had been Peter Corrigan's ultimate goal, along with BJ, but of course they were not the top of the tree in the overall OCG. Truth be told there wasn't really a single top man, Group being the operative word. A host of separate, yet connected, cells of similar characters who disseminated their goods via a huge network. Safety in anonymity.

—

Three weeks later, just before she was due to vacate her flat, Judith moved into the basement apartment at DI Ralph Chamberlain's house. She had decided that she wasn't going to let the Corrigans control or ruin her life. Ralph Chamberlain was delighted.

"I am not going to become your slave and clean up after you, just to be clear. Can I sunbath topless in the garden Ralph?" she asked with a cheeky grin.

"Absolutely. Come rain or shine" he responded. There were a couple of spots in the garden that were not overlooked, apart from in the house itself. He would be able to keep an eye on her, so to speak, whereas she would be shielded from the neighbours. He was answering her in a flippant manner but deep down he suspected that she was serious and would be out there, au naturelle, as soon as she could.

They had agreed to treat the arrangement like proper landlord and tenant with Judith paying a reasonable rent. They would review the situation in a few months having seen how things went. No strings attached or commitment inferred. They were still a fairly new couple and couldn't really say they knew each other in depth, although Chamberlain still had an inkling that Judith sometimes knew what he was thinking before he did.

He decided to buy more pipes. He didn't want to give anyone, especially his boss, any further opportunities to make fun of him and his Holmsean ways. He travelled into Birmingham to find a suitable shop and bought 3 pipes. Two exact replacements for the one that broke and in a fit of self-generosity, he bought himself an Author Pipe.

Author pipes are one of the largest pipe types, featuring a big bowl and extra thick shank and chamber. With a similar bowl shape to the apple pipe, the author features a slightly shorter shank with a thick, quarter-bent stem. The large chamber allows for a great deal of tobacco to fit in the pipe, presenting one with the opportunity to have a lengthy smoke. Chamberlain could take that on long walks and enjoy his smokes in beautiful solitude.

If he wasn't careful, he would end up with a bottom draw full of broken and burnt out pipes, just as his father had. It was a strange thing but fairly universal that pipe smokers found it very hard to throw away old, broken pipes. They were like old friends, that maybe could be mended one day but never were.

DCI Rebecca Flemming was due to go in for follow up tests for her breast cancer. She would need a discussion with a surgeon as to the best way forward for her. There was the question of body image against longer term health, assuming she had a longer term.

Following her consultation, she had some decisions to make. She had discussed things with her husband, who although was supportive, she could tell was also worried about how she would look if she had her breasts removed. She didn't blame him, it was perfectly natural. They were part of who she was and she was proud of them. However, life had dealt her some cards that were a tough hand to play. Treatment would mean time off work and a stay in hospital.

She had arrived at the car park at Warwick Police HQ and as she walked towards the entrance she had spotted a cloud of smoke wafting around the corner of the building. She walked over to where DI Chamberlain was taking one of his smoke breaks.

"Bad for your health, you know" she admonished him.

"Yeah, I know" he replied and put the pipe in his pocket.

"Bad for your trousers as well" she frowned. She had been aware of this particular facet of her DI's clothing disasters.

Chamberlain shrugged and they both went into the building. In her office, she brought Chamberlain up to date with her medical situation.

"I remember hearing someone say that hospitals are like prisons but with fewer drugs" she said to him when she was explaining what may have to happen.

"We can hold the fort here, Rebecca, so don't worry about that. They can send in a locum if they feel it necessary" he told her.

"Or you could take the role as Acting DCI. You and I both know you are more than capable, even if you don't like all aspects of the role" she said.

"I'm not sure I like *any* aspects of the role, if I'm honest" said Chamberlain.

He was not a desk jockey and didn't feel comfortable having to deal with the Brass, budgets and the Press....apart from his own private journalist of course. He preferred to be out at the coal front. He didn't really like coming into the office at all. However, if it helped his boss, he would do it.

"Well, with both Neil and Peter Corrigan out of the way, things have gone quiet around here. I know, I know...don't tempt fate" said Flemming.

"That's it, you've done it now!" Chamberlain was joshing her, he wasn't really superstitious.

Her desk phone rang and they both jumped, looked at each other then laughed. It turned out to be Judith Webster wanting to ask the DCI out for a girls night out with her and Samantha, 'a friend' she had said. Chamberlain left her to it, assuming, correctly, that there would be a whole load of girlie talk, some about him no doubt.

—

Tom Harris and his girlfriend Mads, started going to ante-natal classes together. He found it rather overwhelming at first but soon settled into the predominantly female group that they were with. He got the usual jokes about him being a policeman and a couple of the women said they wouldn't mind being arrested by him. Mads was good humoured about all the banter, thank god.

Mercifully, things had quieted down at work, other than the impending move of the HQ, so he was able to spend some time getting the spare room ready for the new arrival. It was several months away but people get telling him to get as much done as he could now because when the baby arrived his attention would be fully taken up.

He and Mads both agreed that even if they had known the sex of the baby, they were not interested in stereotypical pink or blue colouring for the baby room. They chose a neutral light apple green shade of white.

———

DC Dixon had made her decision and finished her current relationship. The man in question hadn't seemed that bothered so she felt entirely vindicated. He hadn't made any effort to fight to save the relationship so sod him.

She had confided in her colleague, DC Norrish, who had simply shrugged and said he was sorry to hear it. Not quite what she had hoped but then he was a man, and probably not attuned to his sensitive side. She would work on it. She started making her appearance more appealing, something she hadn't bothered doing before now. She got her hair done, at some cost, and started using a little more make-up. Nothing over the top, just a bit of blusher and subtle lippy. The hope was that Norrish would start to notice her in a different light.

"What are you all dolled up for, then?" he said one morning on arrival at the police HQ.

"Oh...just piss off, will you?" she retorted and stormed off to the ladies room to remove the lippy.

If she had only known that inside, DC Adam Norrish was turning cartwheels and shouting from the top of every high place he could think of but externally he was his usual quiet, self-effacing and frankly rather nervous person. He had a horrible feeling that their latest encounter and exchange of words hadn't gone very well. Why then, did he feel so elated?

Tony Robson was on the phone in the ramshackle cabin he used as one of his offices, situated on what looked like a building site near the Liverpool Docks. In fact, there had been no building work carried out there for some time.

"What the fuck do you mean you couldn't deliver?" he shouted at the phone. He was a tall, thick set man and when he shouted, the walls felt it. He was the sort of person you didn't cross, or refuse a request from. The word 'request' was not appropriate really. Do it....or don't do it. That choice was yours. The consequences were Tony's choice.

"I got there and the place was crawling with Police. I drove straight past" said the voice of the lorry driver on the other end of the line.

"Shit.....Ok, take everything to the second drop. I'll make a call and explain the situation. Make sure you are not seen or followed" he ended the call without any pleasantries.

He paced up and down, as much as was possible in the cramped office, and thought what his next move should be. He lit another cigarette, Marlboro Red was his brand and he had been smoking them since he was 13 years old. It had given him a rough, reverberating voice that commanded respect from the people who worked for him or were associated in some way. It also reflected his personality. Rough, unforgiving, and very, very bad for you.

It was unlikely the police would find any connection to him at Stan Hemmings's workshop but it would be good to make sure. Maybe he would take a road trip....maybe he would pay that solicitor a call, the one Hemmings claimed he had in his pocket, although he was already in Tony Robson's pocket. In fact he knew him very well indeed....Frank Williams.

REFERENCES

Thank you to www.jamaicantranslator.com for the Patois translations.

Extract from Wikipedia...

Jamaican Patois (/ˈpætwɑ/; locally rendered Patwah and called Jamaican Creole by linguists) is an English-based creole language with West African, Taíno, Irish, Scots, Scottish Gaelic, Spanish, Hindustani, Portuguese, Chinese, and German influences, spoken primarily in Jamaica and among the Jamaican diaspora. Words or slang from Jamaican Patois can be heard in other Caribbean countries, the United Kingdom, New York City and Miami in the United States, and Toronto, Canada. The majority of non-English words in Patois derive from the West African Akan language. It is spoken by the majority of Jamaicans as a native language.

Patois developed in the 17th century when enslaved people from West and Central Africa were exposed to, learned, and nativised the vernacular and dialectal language spoken by the slaveholders: British English, Hiberno-English and Scots. Jamaican Creole exists in gradations between more conservative creole forms that are not significantly mutually intelligible with English, and forms virtually identical to Standard English.

Jamaican pronunciation and vocabulary are significantly different from English despite heavy use of English words or derivatives. Patois is a term also used as a lower-case noun as a catch-all description of pidgins, creoles, dialects, and vernaculars worldwide. Creoles, including Jamaican Patois, are often stigmatised as low-prestige languages even when spoken as the mother tongue by the majority of the local population.

ABOUT THE AUTHOR

Simon Ford

About The Author Simon Ford Born in Surrey in South East England, Simon now lives in Devon. For the last 15 years he ran a Music Festival. Now in his 60s he has turned to writing, firstly about his experience starting and running the festival, and now a series of books about DI Ralph Chamberlain.

THE DI CHAMBERLAIN CASES

A series of books folowing DI Ralph Chamberlain and his team of detectives who operate from Police HQ in historic Warwick in the Midlands, UK

The Woodland Path Murders

The first in the series of books about DI Chamberlain and his team, solving murders from their base in Warwick, Midlands in the UK. A psychopath lurks in the woods. He has revenge on his mind.

The Copse Murders

The second in the series of DI Chamberlain novels. Having dealt with one psychopath, DI Chamberlain now has another to track down. This one is out for revenge of the murder of his foster parents by drug dealers.

More coming soon...

Printed in Dunstable, United Kingdom

68476548R00157